BLOOD MOON

NEW MOON SERIES BOOK TWO

BELLE HARPER

ELEVENTEEN PUBLISHING

For my sister Elise.
Dreams do come true and one day yours will too.
Love from your big sister, Belle xx

PROLOGUE: GALEN

I have heard by many that in your final moments your life flashes before your eyes.

That everything becomes clear, that this was the natural way of life and death for humans.

I didn't see my life, only regrets. And there were many.

But saving Lexi, that was the only thing I got right in my three hundred and twelve years. She had awakened something in me, and I'd only just started really living. But saving her...it was worth the pain. It was worth everything.

CHAPTER I
LEXI

My head hurt, and my stomach turned. This was a new feeling. I'd never had a headache before, but I assumed that this was what one felt like—like my brain was going to explode out of my head and there were tiny hammers banging on the inside of my skull, trying to let it out. If that was what being human felt like, then I was glad I wasn't one... Well, not exactly.

I took a deep breath, inhaling a pungent odor that irritated my lungs. Ugh *bleach*. It was so strong, and it didn't help at all with the pain in my head. Actually, it was worse and made my nose burn. I tried to sit up, to move away from the smell, when I felt something warm and hard against my body as I slumped back down beside it. I turned my head upwards against the hard chest. My eyes were still squeezed shut at the pain in my head, but through the harsh chemicals, I smelled *summer rain*... It was Raff. His arms wrapped around me a little tighter, and I felt him stroking my hair back from my forehead. I felt safe, happy, as I relaxed in his arms. This was my comfort. My cocoon of safety in Raff's arms, and I wanted to stay there forever. *He chases away my bad dreams and makes everything right in the world.*

"Lexi, are you okay?" he asked. "You scared me so much. I thought I'd lost you," he whispered into my hair and I felt as he placed a kiss against my temple. Oh Raff, such a beautiful soul. I held onto him, letting him know I felt him, that I was here with him.

I could hear everything around me, and soft talking sounded like a freight train in my head. I reached up and held my temples, massaging them with my palms.

"I'm okay. I just have a headache," I whispered, and then groaned as the words pounded in my head. I lowered my hand down and felt my neck. There was nothing there, but I remembered the pain. The pain felt so real.

"Lexi, you tasted just like...heaven."

It wasn't a dream—he bit me. Galen really drank my blood. He drank the poison from my veins, and then he was sick. He was dying...

My eyes flashed open, the light in the room blinding me, and it felt like it was spinning. The pain in my head was upsetting my stomach more as I wrapped my arms around my middle to stop myself from being sick.

"Galen?" I tried to call, but it came out a harsh cry ripped from my lungs. A lone tear slipped free and rolled down my cheek. Had I been sleeping while Galen was dying? I wasn't with him, why wasn't I still with him? Oh god, they buried him, or he exploded into ash and they swept him away. I wasn't sure how vampires died. My throat was tight, and I felt like I was gasping for air. What was with all the bleach...? I felt like I was suffocating. Oh god, he was like those vampires that explode into blood and goo, and they cleaned him off the floor. He was *gone...* Raff held me tightly, I think he was trying to tell me something, but my mind wouldn't quit buzzing. He was dead because of me, he saved me and now he was gone. I choked back a sob, my throat tight and—

"*Ugh*, I think I'm going to be sick." I closed my eyes trying to stop the dizziness and my stomach from heaving. When I felt another set of hands on me, I gasped. I opened my eyes, hoping to see Galen, but the hands were warm and big. Ranger looked down at me and gave me a sad smile while stroking my hands and face.

"Shh... Lex, you really scared us there when you passed out. Galen is—"

Before Ranger could finish, Galen was there, pushing Ranger aside. My breath caught in my throat. I didn't believe what I was seeing until his cold hands traveled over my face. It felt amazing to have his hands on me. He was touching me, pushing my hair away, tilting my head, checking my neck. The intensity of his eyes burrowed deep within me. I let out a deep, rattling breath and clutched my fist into his sweater so he couldn't leave. I needed to keep him here, I needed for him to be safe. He pressed a kiss to my forehead. I could feel the tears building up and getting ready to spill over. God, he was here. Galen was alive. My body was weak and shaky. My fingers struggling to hold onto Galen but I would use all my energy to hold onto him. I was exhausted as I slumped back into Raff's arms pulling Galen with me. I was surrounded by the three of them, all of them looking down at me.

"What happened? I thought you had..." The lump in my throat was thick, and I couldn't even say the words. I wouldn't. He was okay. He was here, in front of me, and this wasn't a dream. He smelled amazing, like sunshine and cotton candy. I let go of his sweater and reached up to touch his face, to make sure he was okay. I touched his curls, which were all messed up and sexy looking. *As always.* In a blink of an eye, I was in Galen's lap, and my stomach protested at the move. But then he held me tight and rocked me gently, and everything seemed almost right in the world. *Almost.*

"Your blood healed me, Lexi. I don't know how

or why. I could feel the venom. I could feel it eating me from the inside, but your blood was soothing, peaceful as it took over and protected me. It was almost like a blanket, putting out the flames."

Holy shit, my blood healed him. What the hell was I, if I could heal vampires?

"For now, we don't want this getting out at all. We just want to keep you safe until we work out what you are. I have ideas, but I'll run them by Pack Bardoul and see what they can come up with. I don't want to play the guessing game just yet, in case I'm wrong."

I must've been powerful if I could heal a vampire, but then again, I was just as weak to shifter venom, since I almost died. Maybe I was like half a vampire?

I reached out and took Raff's hand. His brow was pinched together, but as soon as I touched him, he relaxed, like he needed to be touching me. I felt that too. I felt so much better with him just being there.

Ranger was so close now, hovering beside us. He had that goofy looking smile on his face, but I could tell behind that smile hid pain. His hand was now resting on my calf, he squeezed lightly and winked at me. I rolled my eyes and chuckled slightly, but my headache didn't like it. I looked behind Ranger, and I could see Alaric and Jett were talking in low voices, watching me. Jett waved at me, giving me a half smile before turning back to his father.

. . .

"WHERE'S MAVERICK?" Why wasn't he here? Ranger's expression turned down, he looked away as I watched his chest rise and fall. When he turned back to me, he tried to give me that Ranger grin, but instead, it came out like a pity smile. *Oh god, what...*

"He shifted after you passed out and Galen was healed. Father told him to shift back, but he ran off. He can usually keep in control of his wolf, but I think this was his breaking point. Almost losing you and... Galen." He looked up at Galen, and Ranger's features softened.

I felt it in the pit of my stomach. Maverick wasn't here, that he had left me when I needed him. Especially when we all needed to be here together. But deep down, I got why he had. That was a lot for him, for anyone.

I was still working out the guys, all their different personalities and needs. Right now, Maverick needed space. I knew him the least, and I couldn't be upset with him for that. I was only upset that the five of us weren't here together right now.

I needed to hug Ranger, he looked so lost. I reached over and pulled him in. He chuckled slightly but didn't complain. Normally, he would have teased Galen about how bad he smelled or the fact that he was practically hugging him too, but instead, he just held me. I could feel his body start to relax in my arms, like he needed this just as much as me.

Ranger didn't say any more about his twin. Maverick had opened up a piece of himself he normally kept hidden. He had showed all of us how much he cared for Galen while he was dying. The way he cradled Galen's body against his, and brushed the curls off his brow so tenderly. When he helped Galen get closer to me. When I kissed Galen. I stiffened slightly. *I had kissed Galen, and I told him I loved him.*

He seemed to sense the shift in me. Ranger pulled away, and Galen stopped rocking me. *Oh my God, please don't bring it up.*

"He has some things to deal with, so he just needs a little time and space. Everyone reacts to stressful situations differently. He needed to run, to process everything," Galen explained.

I remembered that they could all smell my change in mood, and Galen must have thought I was worried about Maverick, which I was. But I was also worried about that kiss. He was my history teacher still, and where do we go from here? Oh shit, Alaric saw it too, he would have. He would fire him for sure now. I could tell them I was just saying something nice, that Galen would have wanted to hear it in his final moments, but that was a lie. I knew it, and I was sure they all knew it too. I was in love with Galen.

We sat there in silence for a few moments. I just needed time to think and not let on what I was thinking. Fuck, it was hard to do that in a house full of shifters who could smell my moods. The headache was still there but had started to ease off. At least it reminded me that I was alive, but did Galen do something to give me a headache when he drank my blood? Or did Callum, when he tried to make me a shifter with his venom? Shit, was I okay with vampire venom or would that kill me too? I didn't want to find out.

I looked around and watched what was happening around us. Jett was now talking with Saint, and Alaric wasn't there anymore. We were still in the living room, and nothing had changed except for the strong smell of bleach and the white rug I was on earlier. It was now gone, and we were now on one of the throw blankets from the movie room. I was glad. That rug needed to be burned, since there was no coming back from that blood stain. Plus, too much bad had happened on that rug, I never wanted to see it again.

"So, while you were out, Lex, Galen here... Well, I think your blood is kinda like taking drugs or something for a vamp—" Galen reached out and cupped his hand over Ranger's mouth, and I laughed. I looked to Raff, who just smiled and nodded his head quickly. His beautiful hair I only just noticed was all messed up and had a little bit of blood in it. My blood?

"It wasn't like that. It just gave me...a boost in my powers. I don't feel exactly like myself just yet, and I think the blood is still going to be in my system for a while. It wasn't like drugs, Ranger." Galen sounded like he was telling Ranger off, but I could sense the hint of teasing in his tone.

I laughed, that was kind of cool. But also scary, what kind of boost in powers did it give him? I was quiet again, and it was nice to be in Galen's arms. I didn't want to move, and I smiled to myself. I liked being in his arms.

"I have to wipe Ada's memory and see what Alaric has planned for Ralph's visit—" I turned back to Galen and pushed myself out of his arms. What the fuck?

Now sitting in front of him, I reached out, touching Raff and Ranger for strength. Galen tilted his head, surprised at my sudden move, but he had to know why I would do that.

"Like hell will you touch Ada."

I felt Raff stiffen beside me. "No one is touching Ada. She's asleep in your bed, Lexi." He rubbed my arm, trying to comfort me.

I glared at Galen. He just said he would wipe her memory. I moved back away from Galen, then away from all three of them when he didn't agree with Raff.

They all just stared at me. I narrowed my eyes at Galen. This was bullshit, and he had to know it was. Yeah, Ada talked a lot, but now, I needed her more than ever. I needed her to know about this whole world, be in my corner, and talk about all this crazy shit with me. He couldn't wipe her memory. He could just fuck off back to his little house, if he was going to be this way. Yeah okay, he saved my life, but I wouldn't have been there in the forest if he hadn't been lurking in there and wasn't being all weird and ignoring me all week. I pointed at him.

"You are not going to take her memories, Galen. Do you hear me?" I felt a hand on my back and jumped at the sudden contact. My heart started racing, I turned, hoping it was Maverick. It was Jett, and I tried to hide my disappointment by giving him a small smile. He titled his head and gave me a smile in return. I let out a shaky breath, and he hugged me tight before letting go.

"Hey, Lex, we aren't going to, *okay*?" I looked back to Ranger, his hand on my shoulder, strong and warm. I ran my hands down my face, my eyes gritty from sleep or lack of. The way he said 'okay' made me feel like this was something that was discussed while I was out and not directed at me.

"Galen." You could hear the pleading in my voice. But it was more of a warning than anything. When they all looked at me, puzzled again, I held my head in my hands. Ugh, maybe this blood loss or shifter venom was messing with me. I could feel my body struggling with everything. I was drained, too much had happened, and I needed some space. Raff moved over and held me. I sagged against his chest and closed my eyes.

"I need to go to bed." Then I closed my eyes as I felt him lift me into his arms, cradling me against his warm hard chest. It felt so good as he walked towards the stairs, and the swaying lulled me to sleep before we even got to my room.

CHAPTER 2
LEXI

I woke sometime after breakfast, my stomach alerting me to the fact I missed a meal. Eating three times a day was something I was still getting used to, but breakfast here could be so good, I didn't want to miss it ever.

The headache was gone, and I was so grateful. I never wanted to experience that again. I rolled over in the sheets, wanting to get up and eat...oh and shower. I smelled terrible. But I also wanted to just stay here, where nothing bad would happen. It was safe here. I curled under the sheets to hide myself from the world. *Wow, okay, I need a shower bad.* I was still wearing the same clothes from last night...eww.

"Hey sleepyhead." My heart sped up a little at the voice, but when I pulled free of the sheets, I saw them and almost cried at the sight. My hand covered my mouth to try and stop myself, but I couldn't hold it in, and I sobbed.

"Jack? Grayson?" I choked out. They gave me those warm friendly smiles that they had given me every day I was living with them, and I missed that so much. They entered the room as I sat up, and at a quick glance, I realized I wasn't in my room, I was in Raff's. They weren't coming to me fast enough, so I scrambled out of the sheets—which were trying to tie me down—and as soon as my feet hit the floor, I ran over to them.

I didn't expect this reaction when I saw them. But they were my first real...well, real anything. Real family, real parents. I couldn't hold the tears back any longer. I sobbed as Jack held me tight, Grayson rubbing his hand on my back, saying soothing reassuring words.

"You're okay, sweetheart, we're here. We're here." I started sobbing louder. "You're safe. We have you."

I felt it in that moment—I didn't have to keep being strong, and for once in my life, I really could let down my walls. I could lean on them, and they would catch me if I fell. I trusted them, that they would take care of me, fix whatever was wrong, and make me smile again. This was who they were, this was why they were the best foster parents. It took compassion, understanding, and patience to raise kids from the system. They did it with these beautiful smiles, big open hearts, and cupcakes.

"I miss you both so much. I want to move back, but also...I also don't want to leave here either. I know I don't get that choice, but I just wanted you to know that I will never forget what you did for me. *Never*."

I was sniffing and then so were they. "We thought we'd lost you when we heard what had happened. We came over straight away. But by then, you were sleeping and we heard what happened with Galen. We've been here, waiting for you to wake up."

They were waiting here for me? Jack wiped a tear from my cheek, and it made me cry even more. His eyes were red rimmed, and he looked tired.

"Let it all out, beautiful. You'll feel so much better. We'll hold you for as long as you need. Even though you're not living with us, know that you are still our girl. We made you a promise, and we will keep it forever. If things don't work out here, you will always be welcome back home, Lexi. It's your home as much as it's ours," Grayson whispered to me.

Well, that just made the tears flow faster, and my nose was running badly. *Crap*. This... I never knew how badly I needed this in my life until now. I needed to get it together, since I couldn't spend the whole day crying. I sniffed and took a step back.

"I love you both. You were more a family to me in those few weeks than I had in almost eighteen years. I want to thank you for that. For caring so much, for...just everything." That set them off again, and we did another round of hugs and tears. When I couldn't cry anymore, I took a step back and tried to straighten myself out.

"I'm going to take a shower. Are you still going to be here if I have one?" They both nodded as Jack swept my hair over my shoulder. It had dried coated in blood, tears and snot... But he didn't seem to care.

"Of course, we will and Ada has been waiting for you too. She's in your room. Go wash, chat, and we'll meet you downstairs a little later." I gave them both one more hug and hurried off to see Ada. I was worried and yet excited to see what she made of all this... well crazy vampire and shifter stuff. I bet she was regretting being my friend now.

CHAPTER 3
LEXI

I opened my bedroom door and quickly closed it behind me. Ada was standing at the window, she turned to me and the look of relief on her face at the sight of me told me how worried she must have been.

"Oh my god!" She ran at me and held me tight to her body. "I was so scared! You almost died, and Galen saved you, then..." I started to stroke her long blonde hair, trying to calm her.

She took a step away as she held onto my shoulders looking me up and down, her nose wrinkled a little.

"You need a shower, so I'll grab some clothes for you. Go jump in, and then we can chat...and like I mean really chat. Because I saw Maverick turn into a big gray wolf while you were passed out, and I have a million questions." She pursed her lips and nodded as she started to push me towards the bathroom.

I smiled, I needed this. I needed a friend who knew what was going on. "Okay, bossy boots." I really did need a shower, I felt so icky and gross. I also knew that once she started talking it would be a while before she stopped, and I was actually looking forward to that.

When I looked at myself in the bathroom mirror, I shuddered. My eye makeup had run, giving me panda eyes. My neck was healed, not even showing a scar from Galen. I looked down at my jeans that I still wore. I could see the wolf bite was healed, but there were raised marks...teeth marks. That was new, since I always healed without a scar. Maybe it was the venom that made it heal like that.

Fuck, did he have to ruin my favorite jeans? I wasn't going to be able to fix these. I stripped off and found I looked the same as yesterday. Nothing had magically changed on me, not that I thought it would. I'd just hoped that maybe I'd have a power, that the shifter venom might have woken something up in me. There had to be a reason my blood smelled different and I healed fast. Oh, oh...maybe I had super speed now. I needed to try it. I positioned myself against the bathroom door and tried to run at super speed to the shower.

When I slammed into the shower's glass door, I heard Ada's worried voice call out, asking if I was alright. I wanted to say I'd just found I now had super speed, but really, I'd just slid on the bathmat and crashed into the glass shower door, like a dumbass.

"Yeah, I just slipped." I heard her let out a shriek before the bathroom door swung open, my hands automatically covering my privates. Raff was standing there with his hands stretched out towards me, his face pale and worried. My heart was racing, and I could see his chest heaving heavily. Now that was super speed. When his eyes met mine, I could see his body visibly relax. He didn't say anything before he looked around the room once, then quickly backed out of the bathroom and closed the door behind him. I took a deep breath and started the shower up. I smiled to myself.

As I FLOPPED onto my bed beside Ada, my stomach growled, but I knew she was full of questions. As much as I wanted to forget what happened last night, I really needed to tell her everything. I just didn't know where to start. I stared at the white ceiling as I felt the bed shift, then her face came into view as she stared down at me with her eyes crossed and a crazy smile. I laughed, "I feel so much better now, thank you" I told her, and she smiled.

"So, let's just get this out the way. Galen is a

vampire," she started. I pushed up on my elbows and quirked my brow at her. She had this funny grin on her face. *Man*, she was taking this so much better than it did. And I guess that was a good place to start.

"Yeah, and before you get all chatty, just know that they can hear everything we say. And I mean *everything*." Her eyes grew wide as her mouth dropped open. She put her hands over her mouth as she glanced around the room. "Yeah, I didn't learn that until a few days after. So when you're talking about one of the guys..." I could see her brows were so high, they were sure to join her hairline, and a blush creeped up her throat. I pulled her hands down, and she still looked embarrassed.

"What? Oh god, what did you say?" I wanted to laugh but I was holding it in, because Ada was a talker and she could have said anything while I was sleeping. She shook her head, as she played with the strands of her hair, then she giggled nervously.

"Ah, you know, last night..." Then she gestured with her head towards the window as she twirled long strands of her blonde hair around her index finger.

I remembered last night... wanted to forget about it too. I nodded, but my expression must have shown my confusion about what she was referring too. She mouthed the word "Saint." Oh god, at the party last night, she'd said that she wanted *some* of him, and yes, he totally heard that. I burst out laughing, now that she knew and I could talk to her about these things, it made it a little funny. I nodded my head, and she grabbed onto my hand, her eyes wide.

"Oh my god, *Lexi*. You should have stopped me. Shit...did they all hear?" I didn't know what to say, so I gave her a slow smile. She groaned as she flopped onto the bed, her hands going to her face to hide the pink on her cheeks. I flopped down beside her, pulling her hands away, she looked over to me and I gave her a funny face like she had given me. I took her hand in mine and gave it a small squeeze.

"It's okay. I'm sure Saint already had a big ego before you said that." I giggled, and she playfully slapped my arm and rolled over to look out the window before rolling back to face me.

"So, they're all shifters? That's what Jett told me when he said I could stay up here. I was stressing them out, but I was so worried when you passed out." I could see her eyes welling up. Oh god, I didn't want her to cry. It would make me cry again, and I didn't want to do anymore crying. Plus I just did my makeup, so I looked like I was okay on the outside, but on the inside... I was freaking out and trying to hold it together for now.

"I was fine, just exhausted." Which was a lie, since I had no idea that I had passed out or why. The last thing I remembered doing was asking Galen about my blood. *Heaven*, he had said.

"Shit." I sat up. Was I like an angel? What else would taste like heaven?

"What is it?" Ada's eyes wandered my face, looking for what was wrong.

"I think...I think maybe I'm an angel. But I don't have wings. *Huh?*" Ada looked behind me, like she was checking for wings that might have magically grown overnight.

"Yeah, you don't have any wings." I tried my best not to laugh and shake my head at her remark. But then she laughed at herself and I burst out laughing with her. It felt good.

Did that even make sense? Were there angels? Like real ones? Or what could taste like heaven to a vampire? Fairies? Oh wow, could I be a fairy? I still didn't have wings. Were those things even real?

Vampires and shifters were real...but then how did I heal a vampire? Shit, was I a demon? Was I a good guy or a bad guy? Should I be like killing vampires? Or healing and saving them?

Oh my gosh. Was I like a vampire slayer?

There was a knock at the door, and I froze in my thoughts.

CHAPTER 4
GALEN

"**F**uck," Jett hissed out.

Yeah, I wasn't the only one that heard that. I knew she would be smart enough to start guessing what she might be. At the moment, it was a wild guess, one that I had been tossing around in my head all night. Was there even a possible chance that she was an angel, or part angel since her mother was human. I wasn't even sure if they even still existed. Her mother was human, and maybe... her father was an angel? A fallen one at that.

I was in service of a witch for many, many years. She was very strong and powerful, and the reason I could walk in the daylight. She had told me of angels and demons. They had existed in all her books, even some of her grimoires mentioned them for spells, but that was as far as it went. She'd never met one, or she'd never told me she had. I'd protected her, a hundred-year service for the chance to walk in the daylight. I was her bodyguard, I protected her from other vampires or anything that wanted her dead. I would have known if I'd met an angel or demon... wouldn't I? I guess they would have smelled like Lexi if I did.

"I have this. Let me go speak to her."

Ranger protested, but Alaric gestured I go. We didn't want this getting out. If other vampires knew what Lexi's blood did to me, they would want her. They would kidnap her, hunt her down for her blood. Her blood would make them truly immortal. We had to keep this quiet.

We had Pack Bardoul meeting us here, we didn't want to tell them over the phone why, but we asked for the scientists to attend this meeting. Alaric invited them over for lunch, and they were on their way. I needed Lexi to stop talking though. If any other wolves were around the property, they might overhear, and then the other packs would find out. It would be then impossible to stop this information from getting out. We needed to keep it contained within Pack Kiba.

I was glad for spring break. At least most of the humans were off on vacation for now, and school was closed, so no chance of it being leaked there.

I knocked on her door and heard her sharp intake of breath. She could sense it was me. I could feel her and her emotions when I was close to her, it was like she was a part of me. They ran through me as if they were my own. This had to do with her blood, and something else that I would bring up when Pack Bardoul got here. I wasn't going to scare her by telling her this new development.

"Come in, Mr. Donovani." I couldn't help the wicked smile that stretched across my face. God, she liked to push my buttons in the hottest ways. I never knew I was into the whole teacher-student role play, but with Lexi, I was into all of her. I pressed down on my hardening cock, something I noticed was always affected around Lexi, and strode into the room like I owned it. Ada sat straighter against the headboard and eyed me warily. She looked at Lexi, then back to me.

"Oh god, are you two—" Lexi's hand moved fast, covering Ada's mouth, and her eyes went wide then crinkled at the edges. I shook my head to deny it, but then realized she saw everything last night. The kiss, Lexi telling me she loved me—one of the best moments of my life—how I cared for Lexi after she passed out, how Mav lost it and shifted.

"We're just great friends is all..." Lexi started to explain, looking a little unsure at the statement of us being friends.

I agreed, adding, "Yes, friends...who like to eat cake." Her smile grew and her cheeks pinked a little. I liked to see her like this, affected by me as much as I was by her, and I could feel that through her emotions. God, I could feel everything she was feeling, and it was making it hard not to go to her and kiss her. If she wanted this a secret from Ada, then I would have to play along. For now. *God, she was just so fucking sexy.*

Lexi made a strange sound, then coughed to cover it. Maybe she was thinking the same thing I was...

"Don't you like drink blood though?" Ada blurted out. She was not the best at internal thoughts, I had come to find. "Can you like actually eat cake?" I ignored Ada's questions for now as I had come for a more important topic.

"Lexi, it would be best if any discussion of what you are is only spoken about in Alaric's office or my home, where no *others* can hear." She nodded slowly; her eyes still pinned on mine. She bit her lip, and my body stiffened at the sight. I wanted nothing more than stride over, grab her in my arms and kiss her. Really kiss her, not the chaste kiss she gave me last night. One that would show her how much she meant to me. That I wasn't just a *friend*. I sure didn't have friendly thoughts about her.

"Okay," she squeaked out, so unlike herself. But then, she was still processing things, and I knew what that was like. I hadn't slept at all, still rolling everything over in my mind. Hers was the sweetest tasting blood I'd ever had. I wanted more. But if I was to feed from her again, what would that do to me? To her? Even though she'd asked for me to feed from her in the past, I knew I couldn't drink from her. It hurt me to see she was in pain from my bite, because I cannot compel her. I'd felt her pain as I drank her blood and I didn't want to feel that ever again.

Plus Ranger was right—her blood was like a drug. I just wouldn't admit that to him. I could see more, hear and feel more. My speed had doubled, and I had this strange connection to Lexi. Shifters could smell her moods, and so could I to some extent, but now I felt her. She was confused, turned on, and a little hungry.

"Come down for an early lunch. Jack and Grayson are down there waiting for you."

That had her moving. "Is Joshy here?" I shook my head, and her face fell. They had left him with another shifter family, since they didn't know what they were walking into when they came. As much as Alaric had protested, I told him to make the call, that she would want them to know. It was important for her that they be here. They were the closest thing to a real family for her, and when you're hurt or in trouble, you want your parents.

Even I knew that, and I wasn't overly close to my parents when they were alive. My governess was more a mother to me and my younger sister than my own mother. She'd been too busy worrying about gossip and the next scandal, too busy attending balls and carriage rides around Hyde Park to care about her own children. My father was even more non-existent in my life, spending most of his time with his mistresses.

"Come on, ladies. Let me escort you down to the dining room," I held my elbows out for both of them. Lexi giggled as she skipped over and put her arm through mine. Ada was a little more hesitant, which surprised me, as she didn't seem too bothered by me being a vampire last night. She tilted her head at my words.

"How old are you? 'Cause you sound like you just came out of a posh movie." She moved closer and finally placed her arm in mine. I didn't get a chance to answer before Lexi leaned forward, her golden-brown hair falling from her shoulder as she turned to her friend.

"He's twenty-one...and totally *posh*." She looked up at me and winked, a playful glint in her eyes as she giggled. It was so nice to hear her happy, after hearing her with Grayson and Jack, it took everything in me to not go to her. Ada just shook her head and laughed, but it had a nervous tone to it. She wasn't fully comfortable with me yet, but I hoped that one day she would be, because she was good for Lexi. And Lexi needed a friend like Ada.

After last night, I wasn't going back to teaching. If I had to choose between teaching and Lexi, it would be her. *Always.* I knew that would be something that Alaric would want to discuss with me soon. And I was ready for it. I just hoped I could keep him happy enough to let me still live here. I wasn't too sure what Lexi and I were, but I wouldn't leave her. Unless she wanted me too.

I started to lead them both down the hallway, and Ada was suddenly more relaxed and full of questions.

"How come you don't sparkle? And like, can all of you walk in the sun? Do you know Edward from the movies? Who else is a vampire? Oh wait, don't tell me, let me guess..." Just before Ada could guess or let anyone have a word, Lexi stopped and pulled her arm free of mine.

"I need a jacket," she said as she started to dash back to her room.

Shit... I didn't drink any whisky this morning, so I was making her cold by touching her. I didn't even think, so lost in my own thoughts.

"I'm sorry. I was so wrapped up in things, I didn't think about warming myself up." I would be lying if I said I wasn't a little hurt. Not at her, just at the situation. Why couldn't I have met her when I was human? We could have had a life together, made a family...children

When I felt her return, she reached down and took my hand, which surprised me a little. Then a feeling of warmth traveled through my hand and up my arm, and I gasped at the feeling. It felt so foreign.

Shit, how was she doing that? I looked down to where she held my hand. It just looked like two people holding hands, except heat was traveling up from where we were connected.

"What... Wow." She pulled her hand free and investigated it, but my hand and arm were still warm as I raised it in front of me. It felt so strange compared to the rest of my usually cold body.

"Well, that's new." I didn't know what else to say without worrying her. She had just warmed me up from her touch, and that was very new development indeed.

"I think I might be a mini heater." She chuckled, and I did too, full of nerves for both of us. I could feel her fear. I tried to give her a reassuring smile, but it failed.

Oh boy...

CHAPTER 5
LEXI

Holy shit, oh mother of fuck... I just heated up Galen's hand. His hand was cold, then it was warm. I was thinking about how hard it must be to hide the coldness and always having to drink to warm his blood up so he could pass as a human, and then his hand felt warm in mine.

I was seated at the table beside Ada, and everyone was talking around me. I was still in a daze from what had just happened with Galen. Like did that really just happen? Everyone was talking, discussing in some code type words what had just happened, and all I could do was stare at my hand, wondering if that was really my power. I had a power—I could warm a vampire's hand.

That was kind of a crap power to have, to be honest. I smelled like a shifter's mate, and I could warm up cold hands. *I was a toaster*. Oh wait, and I could heal vampires. Okay, that was cool, and I was so glad that Galen was still here. That I was still here too.

Ranger rubbed my shoulders as he leaned in. "Hey, Lex. Don't over think it. You did good, okay? That is very special." Yeah, says the guy who shifts into a gray wolf and can hear everything. That was special. Being a mini heater was not.

"Eat up," Jett placed a salad sandwich in front of me, and one for Ada, who was looking very out of her element. I assumed that was how I looked when I first got here... Well, she had more clothes on than I did that first dinner. I smiled at that thought, which had Raff raising his brows at me. Ugh, scents. I gave him a wink. He hadn't been here for that little show. But then he got a better look at me earlier in the bathroom.

JACK AND GRAYSON were trying to engage Ada in conversation about school—where she was going, what she was studying. You know, things your friend should know about you. But I didn't.

"I'm staying local, going to the community college in Port Angeles. I'll be studying criminal justice. Not sure if I want to be a cop or what, but I need to do something, or my parents will flip. I just want to see where it goes.

"I'll be living at home and working part time with my dad. He's an accountant, and I think he wanted me to get into finance, but I just don't like the number crunching. So boring. I'll mostly just be setting up appointments with clients and filing." She shrugged. "Maybe I'll change my mind. I'm still young, and I have plenty of time to decide. But I'll be staying in Watson." She turned and smiled at me. She was staying local, and my chest felt light at that. She wasn't leaving for some amazing college states away, with roommates and frat parties. I honestly thought she would be off to one of them, since she had the grades and the brains.

"Maybe I should look into going to the same college," I told her. Alaric had said he would pay for me to go to college. Well, I wasn't sure if he meant go to campus or not, but it would be nice to have friends, and maybe my grades would be good enough. She smiled as she took a bite of her sandwich, quickly chewing it to talk more.

"That would be awesome! What do you want to study?" I shrugged, since I'd never got that far. I just knew I wanted to get into college. I wanted a degree, get a good education, and high paying job. Just no idea what that job would be.

"You could join me?" she asked, and I smiled, but I had no intention of being a cop.

"If you want to be a cop, Lexi, I could take you for a ride along in the cruiser. In the front seat, this time." Nash sat down at the end of the table. I ignored him, like I'd been trying to every other day, and took another bite of my yummy sandwich.

"Rude much? You don't have to be an asshole, you know." I looked up at Ada and saw her...staring down Nash. Oh fuck. I pulled on her hand to get her to look at me, to break this stare off they were having. She was wary and a little skittish of everyone here, but she had no problems taking on Nash like that. He was the alpha's eldest son, would be alpha of the pack one day, and I didn't want her to go head to head with him right now.

"I'm sure she's ridden in the back of many cop cars," he deadpanned, and I gritted my teeth. I wasn't in the mood for this. *Asshole.*

"Hey," Ranger, Raff, and Jett all said in unison. I loved that they were defending me, but I could do that. I didn't need them to be fighting Nash for me, he was trying to piss me off and I honestly didn't know why.

"The backseat is better than riding next to a pig." I replied with the sweetest smile on my face. Jack covered his mouth, and at first, I thought he was upset, but then I could see the glint in his eyes. He was trying to stifle his laugh, but the others didn't care as they openly laughed. Nash didn't say anything as he stood, his chair legs scratching along the white tiles made my skin crawl. His face was all serious again as he stomped off without a word. I knew he would've said something if Ada wasn't there. I was just surprised he left.

I felt a little bit guilty for calling him a pig, but he started it and that was a low blow. He didn't have to say that in front of Ada. What did he expect me to do...roll over and show him my belly? *Hell no.* I fought fire with fire, and he should've known that by now. I would never bow down to him.

"Okay, let's do something fun. I think Mav might even crawl out of his dark hole and make an appearance." I looked over at Ranger and raised my brows. He was here? Maverick came back, and he hadn't come to see me? My chest felt tight, was he avoiding me?

"I should go home. My parents will be wondering where I am. I texted them, but they want me to come spend time with my aunt and cousins, who are visiting for spring break." I stood up with Ada and hugged her.

"That's okay, maybe tomorrow? Or just text me when you're free, we can hang out. Maybe go swimming?" She smiled and nodded.

"Hell yeah, just no more scaring the shit out of me. Okay?" She gave me a small smile before she turned to leave.

Galen appeared beside her, and at first, I thought

he was going to walk her to the door. But the way he looked at me, I could see it. No, no he wasn't going to do it... He glanced to Alaric, then looked down, his eyes not meeting mine.

"You are not compelling her." He shook his head slightly and let out a deep breath as he looked up, his hands in fists by his side, his body was tense.

"Please, no." He looked over to me, his eyes pleading as if he was saying sorry, that he didn't want to do this either.

"No," I yelled at Alaric, my voice pleading with him now. This was total bullshit. They had said they wouldn't do this. This wasn't fair.

"Wait, is compelling a real thing you can do?" Ada asked, more curious then scared. I grabbed her hand as I glared at Galen. He looked Ada in the eye and nodded, his dark curls bouncing on his forehead, but he wouldn't make eye contact with me. He knew I would be pissed off. He said it. He said he was going to and they all tried to convince me otherwise.

"I don't want to. *Fuck*, I'm so sorry." It was barely a whisper, but I heard the hurt in his voice. He knew this would hurt me and yet he was still going to do it.

"Hey, this is bullshit. You promised. Father, you said this didn't have to happen." When Alaric said nothing, Ranger stood up to his full height against Galen. He was larger than him, but Galen still held more power. Though the one who held all the power here was Alaric. He was alpha, and I would never forget that or forgive him for this.

"Alaric thinks it's for the best that I compel Ada, only so she doesn't speak about us and about last night to anyone outside of Pack Kiba. *For now.*" I was angry. I fisted my right hand at my side and squeezed Ada's hand with my left. That was not what I was promised.

"Actually, that's a great idea. Like, if it doesn't hurt, then I'll do it. You can all trust me, but I can't promise I won't accidently slip up. Sometimes I get talking..."

She looked at me and gave me a sad smile. I didn't want to tell her I didn't trust her with all of this. I did, but what happened if someone forced her to tell them, or she saw one of the Kiba boys and blurted out that they shift into wolves for the whole school to hear? Not only would that get her into trouble, but people would think she was crazy.

"It doesn't hurt," was all Galen said. Ranger was still mad and started pacing back and forth beside us. Raff held my shoulder, trying to calm me. I guessed he could smell I was angry. I didn't even need to say anything for any of them to know that.

"Is it like in the movies?" she asked, and I nodded. I really didn't know, since I'd never seen him do it to anyone and he couldn't do it to me. But I also didn't want to tell her that she was the only one in the room that this would work on, since shifters couldn't be compelled either.

Galen stood directly in front of her, and Ranger was muttering things under his breath that I couldn't hear, but everyone else would've been able. He was close to Galen, watching... I guess I was curious to see this too. I watched as Galen's eyes turned dark, and Ada tightened her hand in mine. I squeezed it back, letting her know it was okay. I'd stop him if he did something like wipe her whole memory.

"Ada, you will not speak to anyone about what you saw last night," Galen said in this strange voice, all calm and steady. When he didn't go further, Ranger spoke up.

"You can't stop there. She won't be able to talk to us at all."

Galen continued, "You can only speak to those present here today, and Pack Kiba members. But only if it is safe to do so..." Galen hesitated, I guess waiting for further instruction from Alaric, but Ranger grabbed Galen by his sweater.

"That's enough," Ranger demanded. I could feel the power in the room. It was rippling in waves now, and I felt my chest tightening like all the air had left and all I could feel was tingling against my skin.

"Stop," Galen hissed. I startled from the sudden change in Galen. I knew he would never hurt me, and he seemed just as upset as we were about all of this. He was mad and on edge. Ranger was really pushing him.

"Ranger," Alaric warned, his voice just as powerful in the room, I could see the way Ranger's shoulders sunk at the weight of his father's alpha tone.

"No, this is bullshit—"

"I said. Stop. Talking." Galen was really mad at Ranger. There was a pause, nothing happened and we all just waiting for Alaric or Galen to say or do something. Eventually it was Alaric who spoke.

"That is fine, Galen. That should be enough," Alaric finally called out. Galen closed his eyes and dropped away from Ada, and that was it. The feeling in the room lessened and I felt like I could breathe again as Ada smiled.

"That wasn't so bad. It was actually really cool. This way, you know I can keep the secret and help Lexi too." I hugged her. I didn't want to let her go, but her parents and family were waiting for her at home, and that sounded really nice to go to.

Jett offered to walk her to her car. She turned and wiggled her brows and winked at me. I chuckled and just shook my head. She'd probably get herself a shifter boyfriend before the end of summer. Hell, the end of spring break.

CHAPTER 6
LEXI

Jack and Grayson needed to get back home, but they promised that they would come over during the week and bring the boys, all three of them. I would get to play with Josh, and we could even watch his cartoons in the movie room. I was betting he'd love that. Maybe they would let him watch one of those Batman action movies, or that *Avengers* one, not that I was into them or had seen any, but I'd reckon he would love that.

Ranger was acting weird, and I wasn't sure if it was because Alaric made Galen compel Ada and he was still mad, or that Maverick wasn't down here.

We were waiting for him. Jett had gone up and spoken to him after Ada left. He let us know that Maverick was coming down, and just to give them a few moments. I couldn't wait to see him, I wanted to hug him and make sure he knew everything was okay.

We were going to watch a movie of my choice... again. Ranger didn't even tease me when I said I wanted to watch *The Kissing Booth*. I'd heard it was one of those movies you had to watch, plus...a romantic movie, with my three boyfriends...and Galen. Maybe some kissing...maybe some touching? I really needed that after last night. I just wanted to get back to normal.

Well...what was recently normal.

I nestled into Raff's lap; his arms wrapped around me. I watched Ranger mess around getting everything to work and started up the popcorn machine. I was in love with the popcorn machine, and after living here I didn't think I could ever not have a popcorn machine. Popcorn was the best.

"Hey, how are you doing now?" Raff asked. I didn't really want to be asked that over and over, so instead, I turned in his arms and kissed him. I felt like I hadn't kissed him in forever. Yet, it was only last night. He was so good at kissing, and it always thrilled me a little to know I was the only girl he'd ever kissed. His tongue swept over my bottom lip before he nipped at it. He smiled down at me when I pulled away.

"I take that as good." He winked, then that kiss just wasn't enough. Raff smiled as I turned in his arms and straddled him.

"I'm so much better now." This was helping me to forget everything. I ran my fingers through his hair, messing it up a little. He chuckled deep in his chest, and I could feel that right through my body. "Mmm...that felt good." I rubbed myself against him slowly, and he growled lightly as he gripped my ass.

"Stop teasing me," he whispered, but I knew he didn't mean that when that devilish smile appeared. God, he was gorgeous. I leaned down and captured his mouth with mine.

Every time I kissed Raff, it always felt magical, like that feeling you get from your first kiss—the butterflies, the racing heart. I got to have it over and over again with him. The way our bodies moved, it was like we were in sync with one another. His hand traveled up my back and cupped the nape of my neck, wrapping his fingers in my hair. He pulled my head back to get better access to my neck, and I moaned. God, I was horny. I didn't think I could ever not be horny around Raff. Around them all.

A throat cleared, and the haze of lust around Raff and I broke enough to see Galen and Jett standing next to a very troubled looking Maverick. His hands were in his jeans pockets, his body hunched over. He was barely meeting my eyes with his, which were covered by some of his hair.

"Maverick." He looked like a wounded animal. I jumped up out of Raff's lap and went straight to him. When his green eyes met mine, I could see they

45

were rimmed with red, like he hadn't slept. When he didn't move, I pushed my hands through his arms and wrapped my arms around him. *Oh, Maverick.*

I felt his hands slowly wrap around me, then they tightened, and I could feel his heart racing. His head rested on mine as he breathed me in, and it made me smile. I didn't like seeing him like this. He was usually so put together. I felt his lips on my forehead and knew I needed him to come and lay down with me, with all of us. I needed them all surrounding me, close.

"Let's make a nest of pillows, and we can all snuggle." I considered the fact that Galen might not want to do that. He'd been close to us before, but then for past week, he had been missing. Plus the whole kissing and 'I love you' still hung in the air. We hadn't spoken about it. *Yet.* But Maverick moved to grab some blankets, Galen grabbed more pillows, and I was so happy. Jett came and sat down beside me, and I laughed.

"Yeah, that spot is taken," I teased as I pushed him away. He rolled away onto the floor, holding his hand over his chest with a look of mock hurt on his face, and I laughed. It felt good, we would forget all of this and move on like nothing happened. Everything was feeling right again. Raff quickly took his place and hugged me, Galen lay on the floor, his head practically in my lap, and Maverick was on my other side, holding my hand. Now we were just waiting on Ranger.

"Ranger, what are you doing?" I could see him pacing now, and it was a little unlike him. His head was down and his hands were twisting together nervously. Everyone was here, we were ready, and the popcorn was popping, but Ranger was acting so unlike himself. He did take the compelling thing badly, and I never checked in with him after. I was upset with Galen, for lying but I knew he didn't have a choice. I thought Ranger was upset on my behalf. But maybe he was upset for not being told the truth by his father.

"Hey." I got up and went to him. He watched me, his eyes glassy, tears threatening to spill. Fuck.

"Hey, it's okay. Talk to me." I ran my hands up his chest and touched his cheek lightly. He opened his mouth, then closed it, but he didn't say anything.

"Ranger, it's okay. It's not your fault. There was nothing you could have done. Father makes his own rules, and you can't blame Galen. It's part of the contract for being here with the pack. If he went against Father, you know he would have no protection and would have to leave." Maverick was behind me now, his hard body pressed against mine. I wrapped my arms around Ranger's neck and pulled him down to kiss him. It was small and chaste, but he kept his eyes on Maverick.

Okay, maybe this was weird for him because his brother was touching me too. I'd kissed them both in front of each other, but touching them both...this was a first.

"Ranger?" Galen sounded concerned as he moved over to us. "Talk to me, I didn't mean for this to upset you so much, I'm sorry for the way I reacted."

Ranger's eyes were huge and he opened his mouth, but again no words came out. Then a lonely tear fell, and I could feel my own eyes start to prick with tears. This was really upsetting him, and my heart was breaking. I knew his father didn't seem to trust Ranger with much, I had noticed that since I'd been here, but if he could see him now... He was breaking, and it hurt me so much to see him like that.

He didn't say anything. It was if he couldn't speak. Wait, *wait*...

"You said for him not to ta—" A hand was placed over my mouth before I could get the word out as everyone in the room stared at Ranger. It was Jett's hand that was stopping me from saying anything more. I had no idea where he came from.

"Office now." Galen's voice was very teacher like at that moment as he ushered us all from the movie room and down to the big office of Alaric. We all busted through the door, and Alaric and Nash looked like they were about to attack us.

When they saw the looks on all our faces, Alaric stood up and called out, "Family meeting."

CHAPTER 7
LEXI

Lyell entered the office and closed the door behind him. Everyone turned to Galen and Ranger, because Galen was still holding onto Ranger's shoulder as he watched me. I could still see Alaric looking between Galen and me. I knew he didn't like the fact that there was something between us, that I was playing with the idea of bringing a vampire into my relationship with his sons, but now was not the time for this.

"Speak," Alaric said as he took a seat.

"I believe that when I was compelling Ada, I have also compelled Ranger. I told him not to talk and now..."

All eyes were on a very quiet Ranger. Ranger grabbed his throat and said nothing.

"Is this true?" Alaric got up from his desk and made his way over to his youngest son. Ranger just stood there. His mouth opened, but again, nothing came out. No words.

"How?" I heard whispered from beside me. Nash was watching, and he looked uneasy. I wanted to smile. Maybe Galen could compel him to be nice. But this was about Ranger. This wasn't right. Galen couldn't compel shifters, he'd told me that. He also couldn't compel me.

"It has to be Lexi's blood. I can still feel it. It makes me stronger in every way."

"You're right—it's my blood. It has to be." I looked to Galen, and I could see the wheels ticking over in his head. Everyone in the room looked to me.

"Wow, do you think it's her blood, Galen?" Jett asked, stepping closer to and looking at me with curiosity.

Galen gave me a puzzled look, and cleared his throat.

"I didn't say that," he told me, and he looked serious about it too. What the hell?

"Um, yeah you did. Just then. You said it has to be my blood, it makes you stronger."

Everyone looked at me again, and then back to Galen.

"What?" I felt uncomfortable with all of them staring at me. Their expressions making me feel a little uneasy. It wasn't my fault this happened. I didn't know what I was or that this could happen, so how was I to know Galen could compel Ranger.

"No, he didn't, Lexi." Raff held my hand tightly. "Galen didn't say anything about your blood. You did."

My legs felt heavy, and I swayed a little. Raff pulled me to a chair and dragged me into his lap and held me tight. Alaric was pacing the large room, and Galen was staring at me like I was crazy. Everything was so messed up. Yes, Galen did say that. He said it had to be my blood. Shit, was I going crazy and hearing him in my thoughts?

"Think about something," Lyell spoke up from beside Galen. "Galen, think about something, anything." Galen raised his brow, then his eyes found mine. I moved closer into Raff. This was so messed up, what the hell did Lyell think was—

"Lexi can you hear me? Can you hear my thoughts?" I could hear Galen, but...but his lips didn't move.

My breathing sped up, and I sat up, looking around at everyone.

"Holy fuck." Maverick gasped as he moved closer to me. "You heard him, didn't you?" I swallowed the huge lump in my throat as I nodded. *I did.* How the fuck did I hear that?

"Yes," I squeaked out, and Raff tensed behind me. Oh my god, was I going to always hear his thoughts? Was this a new power? Would I be able to hear others' thoughts? Did I even want to?

"Fuck," I hissed out.

Alaric cleared his throat, bringing the attention of the room back to him.

"Galen, get Ranger to speak once again. We will figure out what is happening and why Alexis can now hear your thoughts." Alaric didn't seem worried or maybe he was good at hiding behind that alpha tone of his.

I could feel the change in the room almost instantly as Galen turned to Ranger.

"Ranger, you may speak now." I heard Ranger gasp and grip at his throat.

"Fuck, this... I never want that to happen again." Ranger pointed his finger at Galen as he took a few steps away from him. "I wanted to speak, but I just didn't know what was wrong with me. I just knew I couldn't speak. I couldn't form words. I never want to be compelled again." Ranger made a wide berth around Galen as he walked over to me.

"I think we should test this out further. Can you compel Lexi?" Lyell asked.

Fuck you, Lyell. He was so quiet, I just assumed he was shy and sweet. But now he wanted to use me as an experiment? Hell no.

"Yes, that's a great idea, Lyell." And of course, Alaric thought that was a great idea. Though, I could tell Galen wasn't happy about this as well.

"I'm sorry, sweetheart." His lips didn't move, that was just for me. Okay, so maybe that was kind of cool. I shrugged like I didn't mind and gave him an

encouraging smile, to let him know I wasn't upset with him. Just this situation.

"Fuck, did he just talk to you in your head again?" Ranger held onto my hand, and I turned to him. His eyes roamed my face, and I could tell he was really worried about me. I just nodded, since I didn't want to say it out loud. It would make it...less special. Because this was special... But this was also just a dream that I was going to wake up from, right?

Galen's eyes were so dark as he got down to my level. That feeling on my skin happened again. But this time, I liked the tingles.

"Lexi, you will stop hearing my thoughts," he said in that strange voice. I laughed. At least he didn't ask me to bark like a dog or act like a chicken. Because that would be something I would do.

"Okay," I said, not knowing what I was supposed to do or say. The pressure in the room died down, and Galen's eyes returned to his beautiful hazel ones.

"I don't believe for a moment I can compel you, and even if I could, I would never do it. Even with orders. I'll be more careful with my thoughts around you, and I'm sorry if you have heard anything you didn't want to."

I thought back to earlier when he said I was *fucking sexy* in front of Ada and she never said a thing. Holy crap. Reading his thoughts was...kinda cool, but could also be a curse. I might hear something I didn't want to. I didn't know if I liked the idea or not yet.

"Thank you, and yes, I totally agree he is annoying." I smirked and gave him a wink. Galen just laughed, and the sound gave me butterflies. He was so sexy and that laugh had me melting into Raff.

Everyone started talking around us, but I just watched Galen, his eyes never leaving mine. His hands were warm on my legs, so he must have warmed up. I liked his hands touching me. I wondered if I could tell him things too. *I think you're sexy.* He didn't even blink at it.

He smiled. *"Are you trying to tell me something?"*

I just laughed, and his smile grew wide. Oh yeah, I was trying to tell him something alright, but maybe some thoughts were best kept secret. Especially with the way he looked at me now, as if I was the most beautiful woman in the world... I really wanted to kiss him.

"Galen, try to compel Lyell. I'm curious if this was a once off." Alaric's voice was always so loud and scary and it shocked me out of my thoughts... oh crap he probably could tell what I was thinking... that was *weird*. Galen winked at me before he stood up and went over to Lyell, who stood taller than he normally would. I was happy it was going to be him. Payback, bitch!

"What do you want me to do?" Galen asked Alaric.

He just waved his hand and said, "Something we can all see this time."

I saw the wicked glint in Galen's eyes before he turned back to a very worried looking Lyell. Oh, this was going to be interesting. Then the room felt tight again as the power Galen held came out to play. I didn't think I would ever get used to it.

"Lyell, you will strip down and shift into your wolf form...and chase your own tail until your father tells you to stop." Galen took a step back, and I could see Lyell rip his shirt off. Dang, he had a nice chest. I wasn't expecting that from—

Wow. I squeaked and I turned away when he dropped his pants. I could hear Ranger laughing from beside me. I reached out and slapped his arm, but then everyone was trying to hold back a laugh. Even Raff behind me laughed, his chest was rumbling with it. I looked over, and there was a gray wolf who was chasing his own tail.

My eyes widened at the sight. *Oh shit.* Then the realization hit me. I had just made Galen the most powerful vampire on earth. I didn't know how I felt about that. I looked over to Alaric and saw he was watching me before his eyes flicked back to Lyell, who had caught his tail in his teeth and was trying to chew it off. My eyes widened as I flinched. Wouldn't that hurt?

"Enough." Everyone in the room shrank down an inch as Alaric's voice boomed in the room, bouncing off all the walls, the power behind it affecting everyone but me.

"Shift back now, Lyell," Galen said, compelling him again. I looked away as Lyell shifted back to his human form. It was something I wanted to see again, but not with him. With Raff, Ranger, and Maverick.

"This is very serious. No one is to talk about this outside of this room. If Lexi was to get into the wrong hands..." Alaric didn't finish. He didn't need to say anymore. We already knew just then how powerful my blood really was, and how much danger I was going to be in if anyone found out.

CHAPTER 8
RANGER

I'd never felt more wary of Galen than I did now. Yeah sure, I liked to fuck with him at school and at home. I was the only one who did, since everyone else was too scared of him and mostly avoided him. But he could do anything to me now... he could kill me. Although I knew he would never do that. He loved it here and wasn't about to fuck that up by hurting me. Plus, I honestly think he liked the fact that I messed with him. I gave him a little fun in his boring life. And he was very much in love with Lexi, and it was clear she was too. So he wouldn't want to hurt me if he wanted to join our little family. Lexi wouldn't allow it.

It was my wolf—who had never been rattled by Galen before— was now all out of sorts about what had happened. How long would he be able to compel me? *Shit.* I didn't even realize he had done it to me. It had been like there was a little voice in my head that told me not to talk when I wanted to, and I'd listened to it without question every time I tried to open my mouth to speak.

I would never shift in front of a human again, as I don't want them to have to go through that after I messed up. And yeah, I had messed up in the past— a lot—and Galen had to come in and fix it. I felt horrible that those people had to go through that. *Would still be going through that.*

Nash approached me as I paced on the lawn beside the edge of the forest. It was late afternoon now, and I needed to shift and run. I needed to think, and my wolf was pacing just as much as I was. I was surprised I had held it together this long after everything that had happened.

Not just getting compelled by Galen, but from almost losing her. I never knew what love really meant until I almost lost her, and I knew I loved her. I loved Lexi with all my heart, and I would do anything to protect her. She was my mate, and I almost fucked that up.

I'd told Callum I wouldn't be his packmate anymore and I wouldn't be sharing Lexi with him, but never in all my years did I think he was capable of that. He almost took that away from me. He almost lost me my own mate.

His rage, his jealousy... She called to him as much as she did all the shifters, and I knew he was jealous that she'd chosen me, but this was... I didn't think I could ever forgive him. He was my best friend, had been since we were pups, but fuck.

I know I had been in the wrong too... It was my fault this happened. I didn't even think twice about throwing him away just so I could be Lexi's mate. God, I was such a dick. I didn't even really give him a chance to win her over. Or to have her meet him properly and maybe have her get to know him, the way I knew him... well I thought I did.

But that didn't give him the right to bite her, to give her his venom. He should have fought with me, not her. Did he think she would choose him if she was a shifter? I didn't understand why he did that. And I would never understand, because if I saw him, I would hurt him. *Shit, I would probably kill him.*

I could never forgive myself for what I did. It was my fault that Lexi almost died.

———

PACK BARDOUL HAD ARRIVED after all the fun we had with Lyell in the office, and yeah, I was calling that fun. If I said it was anything else, I might just shift now and destroy my clothes and all the strength I was using to keep myself together for Lexi right now.

I was trying to not be worried at all the power Galen now had. He couldn't be killed by our venom with Lexi around. Shit, he was now indestructible. I guessed for Lexi, that would be good, since he could protect her from so much more than we could as shifters.

"Do you think she'll be long?" I asked Nash, he was an asshole this morning, but I didn't have time to care about that.

"Not long, they're at Galen's place," he said, making sure not to give anything away. He watched me—fuck, they all watched me like I was going to explode.

"Fuck it, I'm gonna go for a run now." We were waiting for her—Raff, Mav, and I. She wanted to see us shift before we went on our run, and I really wanted her to see me before I shifted. I was so excited that she asked me, but I needed it too much to wait.

"I'll wait here and let her know you'll be back soon," Jett said as he walked over to us, and I hesitated. He'd been interested in Lexi when she first moved in, and now, he seemed to hang around her more than I liked. But he was just her friend and following fathers orders, so I didn't have to worry. Right? *Fuck,* I gotta stop this over thinking shit, it had my wolf even more on edge. And I needed to control him better, for me, for Lexi... for everyone around me.

I nodded to Jett, as Raff started to strip. I guessed I wasn't the only one needing this.

"Wanna race?" I challenged him. He was fast, superfast in wolf form. He cocked his head and smirked. Yeah, it was on. Mav wasn't as enthusiastic about going for a run now, since he'd been running most the night. I didn't care, serves him right. If we were going to be Lexi's mates, then he needed to come with us. This was good for bonding, Father had said earlier we needed to bond together for our mate. That it helps with jealously.

"Can you give her this?" Mav sighed as he started to strip down. I watched as he passed over a green throw blanket he'd swiped from the movie room and what looked to be a tablet. Jett took it without question and nodded.

"What's that?" Did he get her a gift? I didn't get her anything, not that I had time to just go down to the shop and get her something, when so much shit had been going on.

Raff moved closer to take a look at what Jett was holding.

"It's just a Kindle, and it has some books that I downloaded for her in there." Mav just shrugged if it was nothing. Jett started to play with it and laughed.

"It's full of shifter romance books." *What?* Everyone started laughing.

I'd never seen Mav get embarrassed before, but he turned pink *all over*. He didn't say anything he just turned and shifted. I chuckled after him.

"Oh, you totally wanted Jett to give it to her.

Even your wolf is blushing," I teased Mav. He turned his head around and snapped his teeth at me and growled. It didn't stop me from laughing again. Raff had already shifted, and I was the last. This was a first. I smiled to myself, see I could hold it together. I was stronger than I gave myself credit for.

On all fours I could see Mav and Raff already racing ahead of me. Fuckers didn't even wait. I was hot on their heels, but Raff was too quick. I never expected him to be, but I guessed with his smaller size, he did have the ability to move more swiftly. Not like a few weeks back, when we tracked him down...he wasn't as fast then, but he didn't know the forest here as well then. But I didn't want to think about that now—what we did to him. That was messed up, and I was so grateful he'd forgiven me. I knew I didn't deserve his forgiveness, but I had fallen for Lexi just like he did, and he was a much bigger person than I was and would ever be.

I pounced onto Mav's back, and he turned, snapping at me until he lost his footing and tumbled. I didn't wait to see what he was going to do as I took off after Raff. I couldn't see him, but I could smell him... and Saint. I turned to the left, just as a huge gray body barreled into me. I flipped and tried to pin Saint, but he was too quick and was off again, obviously headed towards Mav.

I knew the pack were on patrol here after last night. I still wasn't sure what Father had planned for

Callum. *Fuck*. He would be punished, and I didn't know how I felt about that. I slowed down my steps until I was turning and heading back. He would be punished, and it was all my fault. I should have tried harder to get him to wait, to understand that she needed time. I shouldn't have told him that I was breaking the packmate bond we had. The guilt I was feeling starting to eat me up from the inside.

When I came out of the forest, I could see Lexi on the green throw, and she was laughing at something Jett was saying as she held the Kindle in her hands. She reached out and touched his shoulder, and he moved closer to her. *Too close*. I felt a ripple of jealously, and my wolf sensed it too. Jett was flirting again, with *my* mate. I saw nothing but red as my wolf took over and raced towards him.

CHAPTER 9

LEXI

It was awkward being in Galen's house with so many other people. It brought back memories from the week before... when it was just Galen and me, and the almost kiss. It didn't help having Alaric and two of the medical people in the living room messing up that nice memory. One was a woman, and she seemed nice. Up until she said, "I think it's best we do a full physical exam." Then I didn't like her anymore.

Galen seemed to sense this and told me everything was up to me, that I didn't have to do anything I didn't want to. I guessed this was a way to find out if I was a fairy or angel as I'd suspected, but now, I was starting to fear the answer. Maybe I didn't want to know. I'd lived almost eighteen years not knowing I was different. What was a few or ninety-nine more years?

Everyone was staring at me, waiting for an answer, in the end, I nodded. Let's just get this over with.

"You can use my room, for privacy." Galen showed us to his bedroom, and I followed him in. It wasn't as big as mine, but it held dark wooden furniture. The bed was a king size like mine, but that was a far as similarities went. His comforter was a royal blue, and his walls were the color of the clear blue sky. Apparently, he liked blue in all its shades.

"Here sorry, I'll just get out of your way. If you need me, just let me know." He squeezed my arm and gave me a gentle smile.

"Just whisper my name, and I'll be in here straight-away if at any time you don't want this to continue."

I nodded, and that smile grew bigger. I liked that he could talk to me in secret. It felt special, just something that was for us. I just wished I could speak back to him. He closed the door behind him as he left, and I turned back to the woman.

"This won't take long, sweetie." I rolled my eyes. It better not if she was going to be calling me 'sweetie.' I was missing out on watching my sexy boyfriends strip naked and turn into wolves for this.

I WALKED across the green lawn to where I could see Jett standing, holding a green blanket to his chest and a huge beaming grin aimed at me. I couldn't help but return it. I felt light and free, as I started to also skip over to him.

"I didn't think he would actually let you leave alone." I looked around, and my heart sped up. What the hell, was Callum out here?

"Oh, fuck. No, I meant...never mind. I just thought a certain vamp was glued to your hip is all. He's always one step behind you." Jett's eyes went wide as he looked over his shoulder and back to me, then he shrugged with a smile. "Thought he was stalking me now...you know. 'Cause I'm the hot brother." I laughed. He knew how to make me smile.

"Did you know, you're so vain. Like that song." Jett just winked, flexed his biceps, and laughed. I punched him in the stomach, but dang, that hurt. I waved my hand, trying to get the tingling pain to go.

"Stop hurting yourself, *weak one*, and I would have you know... I only check myself out a hundred times a day." he teased again as he spread what I now saw was one of the green throws from the movie room onto the lawn.

"The grass is a little damp. Here you go, my lady. A Kindle filled with very inappropriate books my brother thought you would enjoy." I held the Kindle tablet in my hand. Jett turned it on to show me. I started looking at the titles and covers of the books and laughed.

"Oh my god, Ranger is such a dork." I looked up to Jett who was quiet, but when the grin spread across his face he doubled over, laughing hard beside me.

"What?" I shoved him, and he stumbled back a few feet, but only because he let me shove him. There was no way I could move him like that unless he let me.

"That's not from Ranger. That's a gift from Maverick, and he loaded it up with books for you. Very *special* books." My eyes widened. Wow, Maverick. I smiled and held it to my chest. It was seriously an awesome gift. The books on there reminded me of some of the books I had recently started reading. I was really liking some of the love stories with shifters, even if most were totally different to how they were in real life. I sat down on the throw and smiled at Jett as he squatted beside me.

"I think it's awesome." I pushed his shoulder as I turned to the device full of happiness—something to help me relax for a while, forget about the last twenty-four hours, and just be a normal girl, sitting in the yard reading—

I gasped when a large gray blur came within inches of me and smashed into Jett. I screamed, gasping for air as I scrambled backwards and tried to get away. I grabbed my leg where Callum had bitten me. Was he mad I didn't change to a wolf?

When the huge gray wolf turned its eyes one me, I heard nothing but the beat of my own heart in my ears. It was racing and I gasped for breath again as I tried to scramble to my feet, only stumbling to the ground. Strong arms wrapped around me.

"*I got you, sweetheart.*" My body collapsed into his arms. Holding onto him tightly while I tried to calm my breathing. Galen would protect me. He had me as I watched on.

Jett was on his feet again, and he punched the wolf right in the muzzle, causing it to yelp as it backed away.

"Fucking asshole, what's your problem? You scared the shit out of Lexi." Jett pulling on his hair and let out a frustrated huff. "Fucking hell, Ranger." My eyes widened at the wolf in front of me. Th...that was Ranger? Why the hell would he do that? Why would he want to scare me? He made a whining sound as he got down to his belly and placed his head in front of me. I tried to move back but Galen still held me. His strong arms still wrapped around me made me feel safe as he turned me away from him. Ranger's big eyes glowed as he looked up at me.

"I...I thought you were him—*Callum*," I said, my shaky voice giving away how frightened I had been, I was still feeling it. I wiped back some tears that had fallen and closed my eyes as I rested against

Galen for strength. Galen didn't say anything, Ranger knew how stupid that was.

When I opened them again, I was staring at an actual pack of wolves, I jumped a little in Galen's arms. The only one not a wolf was Jett. He just stood there beside a really dark gray one and gave me a big smile.

"Your scream alerted them all, and they came running." He ran his hand down the back of a dark gray one, and he didn't look away from me as he did so. I knew then who that was, and I smiled. The wolf's eyes followed my smile, and I was drawn to him. He was magnificent.

"Mekhi?" I asked, and I could see the glint in his eye as he nodded his head. Jett chuckled.

"Yeah, this is Mekhi, and well, you know this dumbass is yours." Jett nudged his boot against Ranger, who was still flat to the ground, his tail was dead still, his ears pinned back. His big green glowing eyes looked like they were pleading for me to accept his silent apology. He made a small whimper sound, and I held up my finger for him to stop. I just needed a few minutes to collect myself, and you know, hope in all of that that I didn't pee myself. I was sure they could sense what I was feeling, and I didn't want them to know I was still a little scared right now. I felt something brush up beside my arm, and I turned to see my red wolf with a wolfy grin.

"Raff." I reached my arm out from Galen's embrace and wrapped it around Raff's furry neck. He was so warm, and soft. I could feel his chest rumbling softly and it was calming.

Jett cleared his throat and I let go of Raff to see what he wanted.

"You want me to introduce the rest?" There were four other gray wolves here I didn't know. They all varied slightly in color, but there was no way I could just look at one and know who it was. It was kind of intimidating having them all staring at me. I nodded, and Galen rubbed my shoulders in support.

"Yeah, that would be good. I don't know how to tell them apart."

Jett nodded and pointed to the far left at the one that had the larger patch of white. "That's Saint, then beside him is...*Maverick*." I felt bad that I didn't know that was him.

He was so pretty, but he wasn't as big as the others, which surprised me. He looked so much like Ranger in wolf form, but looking at him, I could tell it was Maverick. The way he held himself, he was an elegant wolf. I put my hand out to him, and he took a step forward, then he hesitated. Maybe he was worried I would be scared of him. He was beautiful.

"Come here," I pleaded. I wanted to stroke him, to thank him for the Kindle.

I looked down beside me and saw I'd thrown the Kindle off to the side, so I let go of Raff and reached over for it. Galen shifted with me like he couldn't let me go, or maybe he felt safer being close to me, since we seemed to have a large amount of wolf eyes on us now.

"This is Elijah, and you know Noah." *Man, Noah was huge.* I felt Galen's chest rumble behind me, and then Jett started to laugh. I looked around, and all the wolves were looking at Noah, who was staring right at me.

"I think that was supposed to be an internal thought," Galen said. When I looked up at Jett, he just winked as I heard Ranger growl low towards Noah. I clicked my fingers at him, and his ears flicked back to me. He stopped and bowed his head low.

"Ah, did I say that out loud?" I started laughing. "Sorry, Noah. Just, you know, you're big in human form. I don't know what I expected in wolf. It makes sense, I guess. Raff is smaller in human and wolf form." Raff made a strange sound beside me, and the other wolves made whuffing sounds. Jett started laughing even more, and I realized what I had said could be taken in a different way.

I threw my arms up. "Seriously, guys? Do you only think about your dicks? Because from where I'm sitting, I can see them all. If your wolf is matching you size for size..." I cocked my head as if I was actually looking at their junk. I wasn't, but it was fun fucking with them. "I guess dick size doesn't go hand in hand with wolf size. But it's okay, not everyone is blessed in that area." I plastered my fake sweet smile on my face to really rub it in.

The sounds they made were too funny. Galen was laughing behind me. I laughed and rolled my eyes. Guys were all the same, in wolf or human form. Noah and Elijah were the first to run off together, Saint only a few steps behind them.

Maverick's big body landed in front of me, his head resting on my feet, and Ranger crawled in closer to me. I was surrounded by my favorite people.

"You okay?" Jett asked, and I nodded. Mekhi didn't leave, he just sat beside Jett as he continued to run his hands through his dark fur. I wondered what he looked like in human form. I bet he was gorgeous too. I really wanted to meet him.

"Yeah. I wanted to see wolves, and I got more than I was expecting." Jett's wicked smile had me giggling as he waved and left with Mekhi.

"Who's a pretty puppy?" I cooed as I stroked behind Maverick's ear, and Galen chuckled softly in my ear. I thought it would upset Maverick but he just leaned into my hand, demanding more pats. Raff was resting his head close to mine, I leaned back into him. And smiled. I was feeling better now, my heart had slowed to its regular speed and I was surrounded by pretty wolves.

Ranger made another sulky sound, I think he

was feeling a little left out. Well he deserved it after he scared me.

"You're a big bad wolf, Ranger."

CHAPTER 10
LEXI

There was a large, warm body under my head, one covering my feet, and Ranger's big heavy wolf head was now in my lap. I won the jackpot with these puppies, so cute and warm and fluffy. I'd always wanted a pet dog, and now I had three wolves. I didn't think they liked it when I called them puppies. But I kinda wanted too do it again just to see what they would do.

I'd spent the last hour reading from my new Kindle, inhaling their sexy smells, because when they were close, I could smell them and tell them apart. One thing I didn't expect to be doing was pulling their fur from my mouth. Yeah, they were shedding or something. I was covered in fur.

"I can understand why Alaric doesn't allow shifting in the house. Man, you guys have covered me in your fur." And not to mention, they all marked me first before they settled down, Ranger being in my lap because he seemed to really be sucking up to me. Galen told me I smelled like all three of them, but I still smelled sweeter, which I guess was kinda sweet but maybe a little creepy. Like what did I smell like to them?

Galen had left to go do something while I was lazing here, safe with the guys, but my stomach was growling. And it was getting dark now and a little chilly, I needed food.

"Come on, let's go eat." I struggled to get up because Ranger wouldn't let me. He kept pushing his huge head into my lap.

"Come on, I want food. And a long hot bath." I really needed to just relax and have some time alone. Just...to catch my breath. Things had moved so fast, I just needed to reset myself.

Maverick nipped at Ranger's flank, and he yelped. That gave me a chance to jump up and brush the fur from my clothes.

"Okay, shift back for dinner." Raff and Maverick must have been feeling a little shy, they grabbed their clothes in their mouths and ran off just to the tree line not too far from us. Ranger, on the other hand...well.

"You like what you see?" I rolled my eyes as a now human Ranger spun in a circle...completely naked. And dang... Okay yeah, I liked... I liked a lot. He paused and smiled. *Ah fuck.*

"You don't have to tell me. I can smell how much you like it." His brows wiggled, and I rolled my eyes as I started toward the house.

When I got to the house, I could smell what the two packs were having for dinner. We didn't have to eat with Pack Bardoul, since they were having the meal in Alaric's office for privacy. But I was hungry, and I was hoping there were maybe some leftovers.

"My lady." A white bag appeared in front of my nose. I inhaled the scent of burgers.

"Galen, oh my. Yes!" I swung around and wrapped him in a big hug, then snatched the bag from him.

"I got twenty burgers, since I wasn't sure what everyone liked." He shrugged, but that was a great idea. A mixed bag of burgers sounded amazing to me.

Ranger walked into the kitchen, his sweats hanging very low, that sexy V making my body tingle thinking of where it led to. And I knew what it led to... I'd just seen it.

I reached in and grabbed a burger, and Ranger swiped it from my hand. He jumped up on the dark granite countertop and unwrapped it.

"That," I swiped the burger back as he went it to

put it in his mouth, "was mine, asshole. Get your own."

I took a big bite and danced away from him. I could see the playful glint in his eye. He wanted to play, Ranger was always wanting to play and tease but he was too hungry and grabbed another burger.

"Which one is yours, Galen?" I asked as he watched Maverick and Raff now devouring burgers, and Ranger was somehow onto his second one.

"It's okay, you eat. Enjoy." He didn't sound okay, and it wasn't okay if they ate his burger. That wasn't right and he could tell them.

"Shit, did one of them eat your burger?" All eyebrows went up as they watched me go through the bag and pull out a few different types, showing him.

"No, no. I...got onion rings." He held out a different bag full of fries, and inside, I saw the onion rings. I pulled them out and handed the fries to the boys.

"So what do you think they taste like?" I asked, and now everyone was interested in this. Galen smiled, and it was cute as he pursed his lips, thinking.

"Well, they are fried. I've never had fried food before. No *KFC* back when I was human. So, I would think they'd be oily?"

I nodded, and the others agreed. Yeah, there was oil in the fried food, but it was still so good and so not healthy but it was okay to have them once in a while... like every other day.

"Okay, so raw onions taste nothing like onion rings." I popped one in my mouth and started chewing. It was almost sweet, the onion, and I liked them cooked or raw.

"It's soft in the middle. The onion is cooked, so the outside is crispy and tastes so good, but yeah, it's a little more oily." I pulled another up to eat, and a hand reached out and snatched it.

"Hey." It was Jett, and he had a huge grin as he popped it in his mouth and started to chew loudly.

"Fuck off, Jett," Ranger grumbled out, but Jett was like out babysitter. What was he supposed to do? He was always around at the moment, but he wasn't too bad. He was letting us sneak around and do more than we were supposed to. But still, Ranger was jealous and moody with him. Ugh, I thought I would have problems with him and Raff, or even Maverick, because they were my actual boyfriends... the ones I'd kissed. Not Jett.

"I think they taste wicked Galen, nice choice. See ya later." Jett winked and walked up the stairs. I watched as Ranger's face grew tighter, like he was going to explode into a wolf or chase after him and hit him... or both.

"Hey, hey." I pointed over to Ranger, and I felt everyone's eyes on me. "Yeah, you. Stop it, or we'll be having a big talk about this. He's shit stirring with you. You do it too, so stop it."

"He knows how to push your buttons, you know that," Maverick added, resting his hand on Ranger's shoulder. Ranger flinched away from him, but then settled down a little. Raff didn't say anything, he just smiled warily and took a bite of his burger.

"Okay, I'm off for a bath and reading. I need some space tonight. If that's okay?" I looked to Raff. I knew this would affect him the most, as he was getting so used to sleeping with me. He was always there chasing away my bad dreams. He smiled, but it didn't reach his eyes and he nodded.

"That's fine." Was all he said, but you could see he wasn't fine. It hurt me to do this, but I needed some alone time. Everyone needed space once in a while. I just needed to recover and recoup after everything. I was also not used to being around people all the time. It was exhausting. And yeah...I was bound to do something naughty with one of them, and I wasn't ready to jump into that tonight. I might just have to take care of myself and think of them, think of Galen. Oh yes. I wondered how talented he was with his hands...

"Are you sure you want to be alone? The scent you're giving off says otherwise." Ranger wiggled his eyebrows, and I gave a nervous laugh. Yeah, I better walk away from them before I do something that we haven't talked about yet. Because that was going to be a huge step and after the pool... Oh god, that was so hot. Maybe we could go swimming tomorrow—

"Lexi..." Raff moved slightly, and I watched as his hand went to his crotch. Oh fuck, did my scent make them worked up and horny?

I looked at them all, even Galen moved behind the countertop to conceal his lower half. Holy shit, this was some interesting power I had over them. It felt good.

"Oh...sorry?" I smirked before turning and putting a little extra swing into my step. I heard Ranger groan out that I was killing him.

"Not sorry," I yelled out as I started up the stairs with a huge grin on my face.

CHAPTER 11
RAFFERTY

I couldn't sleep. There was a big secret I had been keeping all day. One I was going to tell Lexi in private when we were in bed together. But now, her wanting this space, I had too many thoughts going through in my mind—all my fears, the ones I'd avoided my whole life. *I almost lost her.* I never thought that would happen here, where she was safe as part of Pack Kiba. Alaric said she would be safe and protected here by the pack, but I never knew it was the pack she needed protection from.

I never wanted her to become a shifter. I loved her just the way she was. To see her dying in my arms... That image would never leave my mind, and one I would think about every year. It kept rolling over and over in my thoughts. Even though she was safe now, I had this tension within me. I wanted to go find Callum and kill him. I wanted to rip his throat out for what he'd done, but that wouldn't solve anything. The pack wouldn't stand for that, and I didn't want to do anything to jeopardize my position and all that I'd gained from just being in Kiba—freedom from my uncles and for Lexi to be safe.

Now, without her beside me, I felt alone and lost. I could hear her breathing from here, but it wasn't the same as when I was with her, holding her, feeling her safe in my arms. And of all the nights she needed space, it was tonight. A day I never celebrated but I wanted to privately with her.

Jett had told us that he was going to make sure none of us broke the rules tonight. He promised Lexi that we wouldn't come to her, even if she was having a bad dream. Ranger didn't take that well. Galen had tried to speak to him, calm him down, but he wouldn't listen. He really had it out for his older brother, and when he saw Jett casually sitting against Lexi's door frame, wearing a tank top and boxers, his bare legs stretched out, ankles crossed, and playing on his phone. Ranger saw red and stormed into his room. Maverick followed him in and closed the door behind them. That was when I really felt it... alone.

They had a lifelong bond of brothers, I didn't have that with them. I knew Ranger said he would always have my back, so did Maverick. But they would always have each other's too. If it was down to me and one of them, they would choose each other. I wouldn't hold that against them, they were bonded through blood, but all my doubts and worries were building. I was starting to really see what an outsider, a rogue wolf I really was.

My old pack, they'd treated me like an outcast for my whole life. I hadn't really thought of them at all since I moved in here to the Lovell house. Lexi, she was everything I had dreamed for. Alaric was to be my alpha, and he'd already accepted me as part of his pack. He didn't have to, but he said he wanted me. On my eighteenth birthday, he said there would be a ceremony and I would become a full member of Pack Kiba that night.

There wasn't a huge celebration, there wasn't even a happy birthday. It was the same as every year. And once again I was alone. I knew it wasn't anyone's fault, so much had happened and it just got pushed to the bottom of the pile. But it didn't mean it didn't hurt any less. If anything, it hurt more knowing I had these people around me and I was still alone. I should have told them earlier. Told Lexi, she didn't know it was my birthday. How could she? I never told her the date. I let out a shaky breath, trying to hold my tears back. I closed my eyes and lay down on the bed.

Happy birthday Rafferty.

I STILL HAD THESE FEELINGS, that I would do something wrong, or say something to offend Alaric or anyone in the pack. That all of this, it might not last. He would get tired of me and make me go back to Pack Russet, and I can't go back... They would kill me.

My chest felt tight as I paced my room again. I felt like I was walking on eggshells in this house, always trying my best to please everyone, but I felt like I was failing at every step. I didn't even know how to be a boyfriend. I could lose the pack and be fine, but I knew I couldn't survive if Lexi broke up with me. She was the one thing that was holding me together in this fucked up world.

What if Lexi got tired of me? I was the one who slept with her at night and chased away her bad dreams. I'd never slept as well as when I was with her, and now...now she didn't want me there. Did she still need me? Want me? My chest was tight, and my heart was racing. I was working this up to be bigger than it was, I knew that but I couldn't stop the rollercoaster.

Was she upset that I didn't say anything to Alaric when he ordered to have Ada compelled? I couldn't say anything, he was alpha and I had the least power in that room. Even Galen, a vampire living with a wolf shifter pack, held more power than I did.

I looked out of my window. Galen still had his lights on, and I wondered if he felt like me. He was also an outsider here in Pack Kiba. We hadn't spoken much, even though he had been driving me to school and back, but those rides were more a one-sided conversation. I listened to him, but I wouldn't call us friends, exactly.

He was a teacher and a vampire, but he was more than that to Lexi, and I was still unsure what Lexi wanted. Did she want him as a friend? A mate? She hadn't spoken about it or shown that he was a mate at all today, but she told him that she loved him last night. And I knew he didn't miss those words. No one did.

A knock on my door startled me. "Yeah?" I called out. The door cracked open, and I saw the twins—my packmates.

"Hey, you up? I was hoping we could talk," Maverick asked.

I took a deep breath and returned to the bed, settling myself down as I watched them both do the same. Ranger didn't look at me. He worried his hands in his lap before stopping and looking to Maverick.

I was worried, angry, and afraid. I was sure I was scenting that too, and my wolf started to stir again. I was out of my element here. I didn't know what they wanted to talk about, and it was messing more with my head than I thought it would.

"It's okay, Raff. Ranger here is having some time adjusting to everything that has been going on lately, and I think it's good for us to all sit down and talk. Get on the same page. For us and for Lexi. If we're all doing this, we're in it for life, and now more than ever, we have to be united front. I don't know what will happen tomorrow or the next year, but we all know we feel the pull to Lexi. Even now, I can feel her here." Maverick tapped his chest, and subconsciously, I raised my hand to mine. I nodded.

I knew now was the time to open up, really open up to these guys, but I still didn't know exactly how. Trust was the only way forward. I was nervous to lay myself out to them, but I need to do this. We needed this. I took a deep breath, my stomach in knots.

"I want Lexi to be safe. I never thought I'd have a mate. It was a dream I never saw happening for me, until I came here."

They both nodded, and I felt a weight had been lifted from my shoulders. "Galen is good for her too. I...I wasn't sure at first, but honestly, it makes me feel better knowing she has him."

Ranger nodded and took a deep breath. He must have felt the same nerves I did.

"You're my packmates, and I'm sorry if I've been acting like an asshole around Jett. I don't know why, but my wolf just gets stirred by him, and he is doing it to test me. Today has been long, and all I wanted to do was to cuddle Lex as she fell asleep, but I didn't get that. I've never had that." He sighed, and I felt that too. I knew I was the one who got to do that, but that was before she chose them both. I guessed it was something I'd have to share with them.

"I know she just wanted a night to herself, but tomorrow night, what if her nightmares come? Would I be allowed to go to her? I want to help her. Spend more time with her."

We all sat on my bed talking, laughing, and bonding over everything. It felt good. No, it felt amazing. But I didn't tell them what this day was, no. I kept it to myself. I didn't want to make it about me. This was about Lexi, us and Galen.

All the fears I had about the guys settled. I finally felt comfortable enough to sleep, and with Ranger and Maverick here with me, I could relax. Nothing would happen if I was to fall asleep. I felt their protection. They would have my back.

CHAPTER 12
LEXI

Sleep wasn't so bad, but I missed waking up to Raff and having my morning kisses. Though it was also nice to have time alone, time to think without being worried what scents you were giving off all the time. Ranger also mentioned them all the time. I smiled to myself. He was such a pain in the ass, but dang, I really liked him. I rolled over and looked at my phone.

I got a tiny sleep in... It was only seven am. Shower time, or another bath...? Oh, the bath last night was so good. I hadn't been able to take advantage of the bath as much I wanted. I needed one at least once a day. That would be my new rule, so I could relax and read, have some alone time to myself.

I opted for a shower so I could wash my hair again and shave. I just needed to feel clean all over, wash away all the crap and start a whole new day. The only memory I would have of that night was in my mind and on my thigh. But I was good, this was my spring break, so I was taking charge and everyone was going to have a good day.

I dried my hair and wrapped a towel around my body, I opened the door to my bedroom and noticed instantly that my bed was made and now had a very sexy, half naked guy in there.

"Ranger! What the hell are you doing?" I cocked a brow at him , and he wiggled his brows at me. I shook my head and rolled my eyes.

"Oh, you know. I came to see you. I made your bed for you... You are so beautiful and looking sexy as hell in that towel, Lex. Come here." He patted the spot beside him. I shook my head, ignoring that last part, and laughed. Oh, he was incorrigible. When he wasn't being a jealous asshole, he was cocky and very good at sweet talk. And dirty talk.

"I can make my own bed. You're not supposed to just come in here..." He laid back against the pillows and put his hands behind his head, making himself at home. His eyes slid down my body, which was still wrapped in the towel, then moved back up to my face. A sexy grin formed on his lips as he nodded his head to the space beside him. Oh boy, he was good. He had that 'come here' sexy thing down.

"You want me to join you?" I asked in a sultry voice. I could see the wheels turning over in his head. He wasn't too sure if I was fucking with him or serious. But when he gave me that cocky smile...I could tell he didn't care. He was game either way.

"Oh...well, hello there, big boy..." I started to crawl up the mattress towards him, running my fingers up the inside of his calf to his knee. I bit my lower lip and looked up at him through my lashes. His eyes followed the path of my fingers. He made a sound in his throat, almost animal like, and my mouth twitched into a small smile. I liked this power I had over him.

"You like that?" I asked. He swallowed hard and nodded. I didn't need to ask him, I could see how much he liked it, his boxers struggling to contain him. And after yesterday's naked show, I knew exactly how much work that material was doing holding him in there.

"You want me to touch you?" He groaned and nodded again, I slipped my fingers gently over his hard cock and placed my palm on his stomach. He started to bend towards me, so I pressed him down with my hand and he flopped back again, his abs tensing under my fingers. Fuck, he was hard... everywhere.

"Oh...naughty girl wants her wicked way with me? I want to touch you too. I can make you feel good, Lex. Let me touch you...lick you. God, I want to taste you so bad." Shit, he was making me wet. And I came just to tease.

"Ah...no, I'm good. Thanks for the offer though." I jumped off the bed as I held onto my towel and dashed into my closet, laughing. It took a good three seconds for Ranger to understand what had just happened, and he chuckled.

"Hey, tease." He was at my closet door now. He leaned on the door frame, his hands crossed against his chest, and grinned at me.

I had my bra and underwear on, and was just picking out some blue jean shorts and a black tank.

"I'm gonna have some breakfast. You *coming*?" I asked as I slipped the shorts on and buttoned them up as I walked past him, bushing my body up against his, my tank hanging over my shoulder.

"I was hoping someone would be *coming* this morning..." I chuckled at his response, opened the bedroom door, and started strutting down the hall, putting my tank on as I went.

"Good, come on. I'm hungry." He growled lowly, and I squeaked. I started to run, but Ranger was too fast. His arms wrapped around me as he swung me in a big circle. I laughed and squealed as he started to tickle me.

"I'm hungry...but there is nothing I want to eat more than—" I elbowed him, and he let out a grunt. "I was going to say pancakes, but now I won't make you any."

"Good morning," I said as Saint walked through the door and into the kitchen after me. He had a cheerful smile and winked at me. He was wearing long shorts and a dark tee.

"So, did you have a *good* morning, Ranger?" Saint propped himself on the end of the countertop and looked over at us, Ranger laughing, shaking his head. He'd followed me down, not even putting on any clothes. Shit, I wondered if they always just walked around half naked like this before I came here. Fuck, why does Ranger have to stand there looking like he stepped out of a movie? Those abs... I just wanted to run my hand over them again to see if they were real.

I watched as he pulled out flour and milk... Oh he was still going to make pancakes. I stopped and watched him. I felt a blush in my cheeks, I was getting all worked up, and I bet that was his plan. I quickly turned away, biting the inside of my cheek.

He wrapped his hands around my waist and kissed my cheek. I pressed my ass into him. He was still hard, so I gave it a little wiggle, and he groaned into my ear as he whispered, "You naughty girl. Want me to take care of you? Here?" Oh man, teasing Ranger was just as much torture for him as it was for me. He laughed.

"I can't help that you smell so good and you're sexy as hell when you're frustrated with me. Can I maybe have a kiss?" The puppy dog eyes... Ugh, he was so adorable and cute.

I gave him a quick kiss before turning to see Saint watching us with a big grin.

"Do I get a kiss too?" I glared at him, and he only chuckled.

"I'm going to go check on Galen. I'll be back later." I let them know as I grabbed an apple from the fruit basket. I walked past Saint and shoved him off the end of the counter, but he landed on his feet. He shook his head and raised his hands in surrender.

"I take that's a no on the kiss?" I shook my head, trying to stop myself from laughing. Okay, Saint was growing on me. I turned back to see Saint watching me, or maybe he was watching my ass? Ranger seemed to notice and punched his shoulder.

"We're gonna play some football today, Lex. You gonna come watch? Cheer your boyfriend's on?" Ranger called out as I opened the door.

I paused before throwing my fist in the air and very sarcastically called out, "Go team."

But yes... yes I was going to watch because he said boyfriends and that made me feel all gooey inside.

CHAPTER 13
LEXI

I headed over to Galen's. I knew I needed to speak to him about the kiss, I just didn't want to do it with the guys around, overhearing everything. Especially with Ranger being the way he had been with Jett. He'd been so snappy and rude to him.

I knocked on the front door and waited. I couldn't hear him, either inside or in my head. I wondered if he was even here. After waiting a fair amount of time, I knocked again and tried the door handle. It was unlocked. Huh, I wondered if he ever locked it. I guessed it was a small town, and he was a vampire. Not too many shifters would want to be caught in here with him.

"Hello?" I called out as I looked around the living room. A bookcase in the corner of the room caught my attention, and my feet started moving towards it of their own accord. It held so many old books.

There was a beautiful green and blue stone about the size of my palm displayed on the shelf, all smooth and shiny. I ran my index finger over the top, then up the spine of the black leather book beside it. The gold letters were embossed into the spine, and it wasn't in English.

I heard a sound...footsteps. I froze. Shit, what if Galen wasn't here...or he was dead? And that was why he didn't hear my knocking? My palm pressed tightly to my chest to stop my racing heart. If it was a supernatural person, they would hear me, smell me. *Fuck.* I was so fucked. A door opened and closed. I was on the floor now, trying to crawl towards the front door.

"Lexi? What the hell are you doing?" I gasped and turned to see Galen standing above me, his hands hovering in front of him, then reaching for me. I let out a shaky breath. It was just Galen, oh god. How did I work that up so much in my head? I guessed from all the shit I had seen and lived through. Nothing was as it seemed...especially here in Kiba.

"I was coming to talk to you." I reached up and took his hand. It was cold in mine. He pulled me to my feet, and I brushed the dust off my clothes. As if they even had dust on them, this house was too clean. Even the bookshelf had no dust when I had touched it. He took great care of his home.

He gave me a smile, the beautiful one that he

didn't show very often. He scratched his head, his curls bouncing around. Then he gestured for me to go into his small kitchen. I pulled out a dark wooden stool on the other side of the counter, then jumped up to sit at it as he opened his refrigerator. I couldn't help myself, I peered over his shoulder, thinking he must keep blood bags in there. I hadn't seen him eat before, so I was curious. Did he have a preferred blood type? I had no idea what my blood type was.

"Juice?" He spun around, holding out a bottle of orange juice. I could now see into the refrigerator and it was full of...food?

"Ah, yeah...do you always have food in there?"

He turned back to look at the food I was staring at, and when he turned back to me, he smiled and chuckled.

"Not always, it's a new thing." I smiled at that. Did he buy the food for me? When I didn't say anything, he added, "I was hoping that you would come over and want to eat here sometimes. You're always welcome in my home, Lexi."

He poured the juice for me into a tall glass and pushed it across the counter to where I was sitting. I took a sip, and it was so good. It wasn't that cheap shit. This was the real deal, freshly squeezed.

"Thank you." I didn't know what else to say. I had too many thoughts and feelings running through my mind. So, I quickly added, "For the juice and the offer." There was an awkward silence between us as he put the juice bottle back and pulled out some eggs and bacon.

"Are you cooking me breakfast?" I didn't know what to say, since I wasn't expecting this at all when I came here. I'd nearly given myself a panic attack, and now Galen was making me breakfast.

"Well, I haven't done this in like...ever. So if it's terrible, let me know. But I remembered you liked it when I took you to the diner...and I watched some cooking shows."

Oh god, the diner. I could feel my cheeks pinking at that, my hands going to my cheeks to hide them. I remembered that diner too well. That was when I figured out he was a vampire and I told him I was team shifter, but I knew that was a lie when I said it. God, he was so fucking hot right now with his tousled morning hair and green knitted sweater. It seemed out of place today with it warming up nicely, but it looked so right on Galen. He had on black jeans that hugged his ass.

He rolled up his sleeves and brought out a frying pan from a lower draw. That was when I noticed the scars on his arms, criss-cross scars up both of them. When he cleared his throat, I realized I was staring at them. Fuck. What the hell caused scarring like that on a vampire?

"How do you like your eggs?" My eyes flashed up to see his. I could tell my staring made him uncomfortable, and I didn't want to do that to him.

"Shit, um...fried is fine." He nodded and turned his back on me, hiding his arms more. *Fuck.* I looked around the kitchen, trying to find something to say, when he spoke up, the bacon sizzling in the pan.

"You can ask me." I sat frozen on the stool. "I know you're wondering what happened to my arms. I can hear your heart beating faster, and you're not good at hiding your emotions. I don't often show the scars, but it's okay, you can ask. And well, I guess if you're here," he turned to me, a spatula in one hand, his left arm straight out, showing me the silvery scars on his arm again, "you want to get to know me?"

I tried to smile, but I thought I gave him that sad version of a smile no one liked to see. I nodded.

"Yeah, I was here to talk, since I want to get to know you. I won't ask you though. If you want to tell me, I'll listen. Some people wear their scars on the inside, and no one asks about them because they can't see them. So I would never ask about the ones I can see."

Galen just stood there, his mouth slightly agape. The popping of the bacon had him turning around and flipping it. He didn't say anything, he just stood there staring into the bacon. I guess he was thinking about what I said, maybe wanting to know what scars I hid on the inside. Though he did read my file, so I guess he knew a few of mine.

"You can't hear me anymore, can you?" he asked, and I sat up straighter. No, I hadn't heard him at all.

"It's not there anymore is it? We can't talk like that anymore." I sounded sad because I was. I'd really enjoyed that yesterday. Like when he slipped up in the bedroom and I thought Ada had heard him and I was freaking out.

"I thought it might have gone. I guess this morning was a little strange for me. It was almost as if I was waking up after a bad hangover, and I haven't had one of those since I was a human. I feel a little off, sluggish and tired."

Wow, I didn't realize my blood would have such a bad effect on him like that. I guessed he wouldn't want to drink from me again if that was how he was feeling after.

"I was going to ask if you wanted more, but..." He turned now, a plate full of bacon and two fried eggs on the side. I guessed this was pretty good for someone who never needed to cook. I would've preferred some toast too, but I wouldn't tell him that. He'd made me breakfast. Galen Donovani cooked for me, and it looked and smelled perfect.

"I can't, Lexi. I don't know what else could happen if I drank from you. I can't compel you, and I won't ever cause you pain. I felt so guilty after... I just couldn't stop thinking about how I'd hurt you more than Callum had."

I shook my head and jumped down off the stool.

Galen had his hands covering his face, and he looked shocking, the painful memory hurting him as much as me. Although I wanted to talk to him about what happened, I also just wanted to forget everything and only focus on the positives.

"Galen." I took his wrists in my hands, but he didn't budge when I pulled. He was still powerful and strong. I gave him a moment, a chance to really pull away from me, but he didn't. Instead, his hands dropped from his face. He looked tired, with dark circles under his eyes and a sad expression. God, he looked so young right now. It was hard to imagine he was this super old vampire, when he looked like a lost young man who had lost so much.

"You didn't hurt me. I honestly don't remember the pain of you biting me. I did like when I could hear you in my head. I loved that, in fact. It was like our own private conversation, something that doesn't happen around here often. Maybe if you just drank like a little?"

I didn't know why I was begging a vampire to drink my blood. I just knew I wanted Galen too. In a way, it was our own personal connection. Even if we never were more than what we were now. I wasn't sure if he still wanted me...but this way, he would always have a piece of me and I would always be with him, even just a little.

He slowly shook his head no, but I could see he was rolling the idea around in his head, overthinking everything. I stepped closer to him and wrapped my arms around his very tense body. He sagged a little into me as he wrapped his arms around me. There was comfortable silence for a long time. I knew my breakfast was now cold, but Galen hadn't moved at all and I didn't want to let go. This was perfect, but my stomach decided now was a good time to growl.

"You want to *suck my blood?*" I did my best vampire voice. I didn't know why I said that, but it just felt right to cheer him up. Galen pulled back slightly and looked down at me, and I watched as the corner of his lip twitched up into a smile.

"You know I don't sound like that." I laughed and shook my head.

"You do, maybe you just can't hear yourself. You sound just like a regular old vampire. Is the Count from *Sesame Street* your uncle?"

That had him chuckling, and it was a beautiful sight. He was so gorgeous in this moment. He was beautiful when he smiled, but that laugh had my insides heating up.

"I was thinking that maybe I could take a little of your blood. I shouldn't, but fuck, you're hard to say no to, did you know that?" I winked and turned my neck to him, brushing my hair off my shoulder so he could have better access. The move made him tense up again.

"I was going to draw your blood, you know into

a blood bag, so it won't hurt so much." I watched his eyes as they focused on the racing pulse in my neck and started to get darker. His hand came up the column of my throat, his thumb brushing over my skin ever so lightly. He moved closer until he was breathing me in.

"You smell amazing, Lexi." His cold nose ran up my throat to my ear. I felt him press a small kiss just below my jaw, and my fists clenched in his sweater, holding myself upright at the feeling. I let out a sharp breath and felt his smile against my skin. My breathing grew deeper and I pulled him closer to me. I wanted to feel his lips against mine.

He chuckled as he pulled away.

"Go have breakfast before it gets cold. I'll go get some things ready." Then he was gone, using his super vampire speed to run away from me. I felt cold at his sudden change, which was strange, as he'd been making me hot. I wrapped my arms around myself and returned to my now cold breakfast.

I wasn't hungry anymore. For food that was.

CHAPTER 14
GALEN

Fuck, fuck, fuck. I didn't know what I was doing. I was practically hiding in my basement thinking about how I was fucking this all up. I shouldn't be taking her blood, I shouldn't even be thinking about this. I'd even told Alaric what my plans were for Lexi and school. That even if she didn't want me...I would still quit and take care of her full time. She needed someone to protect her. I quit then on the spot. It was done.

Shit. I was so close to taking her back there. I wanted to bite into her soft neck, to drink straight from her, to spread her out on my kitchen floor and taste her, and not just her blood. I wanted to touch her, bring her to heights she never knew existed. I was so hard just thinking about it, but I couldn't just rush into this. I wanted to do this right, court her, get to know her before things went to the next level.

I could hear her upstairs. She'd returned to the stool, but she wasn't eating. I'd been so close to giving in and just kissing her there in my kitchen, but now I worried I had upset her with my sudden movement away from her. She was so warm in my arms, and I needed the space to clear my head. I'd felt my fangs itch at her scent. I'd felt the darker side taking over. So I'd needed to get away before I did something stupid, before she saw me as that...a vampire.

She looked at me like a person and treated me as an equal. I loved that she took the time to tell me what her food tasted like and insisted I buy foods that I wanted to try. This was why I fell for her... hard. She was so different to anyone I had ever met. I quickly grabbed a bottle of whisky and downed a mouthful, hoping the effects would take place soon. I didn't want her to feel me cold like a vampire. I wanted to feel warm and human for her.

When I returned to the kitchen, she was looking down at her food and took a bite of her egg. Maybe it wasn't my sudden escape from her, and I really didn't cook it right. It had looked the same as the lady on the cooking show. But when she didn't look over at me, I knew it was me and my need to get away from her that upset her. I didn't know how to fix this, so I did the next best thing. I tried to speak to her about something else.

"It's best if you have something to eat and drink

some water." I placed the equipment to draw her blood on the coffee table. When she didn't say anything, I grew worried.

"That's if you still want to, you don't have to give me your blood, Lexi. You know that, right? It doesn't make a difference in how I feel about you if you choose not to. I..."

She glanced at me, and her big amber eyes almost glowed from the sunlight streaming through the windows. All the words escaped my mouth as I froze. Her lips curled into a deadly smirk—deadly to me, because I would do anything for this girl. She jumped off the stool and slowly walked towards me. I watched her as she sized me up, like she was stalking prey.

"And how do you feel about me, Mr. Donovani?" I let out a small groan at the way she said my name. Her hand pressed against my chest as she came closer. Whatever I said was the right thing to be rewarded with this.

"When I told you that I love you, was that only one sided?" Fuck, I loved this side of Lexi, when she took control and she knew what she wanted. It was hot as hell and one of the reasons I had fallen for her. She'd been a little unsure of herself lately, and I put that down to all the changes she had been through, but she was still a little fireball inside.

"No. It might have been one sided...before you fell for me. But I've loved you from the first moment

I saw you, Lexi. When you were in the school office, I couldn't look away. I saw a beautiful, smart, and defiant young woman. But you're young, and I'm much older. I never thought you'd look at me the way you do. I never thought that I could have you. That you would want me."

I knew I shouldn't, that I was too old for her, not good enough for her, but I couldn't hold back. I wanted her, I needed her. My hand snaked up behind her head, and before she could say another word, I took her mouth. This wasn't a sweet kiss, this was primal. All the hunger I felt for her, all the times I wanted to kiss her smart little mouth, this was all of that in one heated moment, and she didn't pull away.

She gasped, grabbing ahold of me, and I pulled her tight to my body. Her hand on my chest was crushed between us, but she could feel how hard I was for her. How badly I wanted her. I licked the seam of her lips, and her tongue came out to meet mine. I groaned at her taste, so sweet, so fresh. We stayed like that, learning each other's mouths, breathing each other in. She rubbed herself against my erection, and I groaned at the friction. I nipped gently at her lower lip, not wanting to draw blood, but wanting her to remember this kiss for the rest of the day. Even though she healed fast, she won't forget what happened here.

"That..." She pulled back, touching her lips with

her fingertips, her eyes moving to my mouth as she traced her fingers along my bottom lip. I felt her index finger touching what I knew she saw there. I couldn't control myself when I was so worked up, and my fangs came out. I watched her expression, knowing that she would see them in a way I didn't want her to. But I couldn't hide my fangs, she knew what I was. And it didn't bother her, it was me that was more hung up on that.

I felt her run her finger along the bottom of one fang, and it felt good, different. I closed my eyes as she pressed hard, I smelled the iron in her sweet blood.

My eyes flew open, and I found her watching me intensely. Our eyes locked, and she didn't look away as I grabbed her wrist to stop her. I pulled her hand back and saw the red beading at the tip of her finger.

"Why?" I asked, but it was a stupid question. We both knew why. I pulled her finger up to my mouth, my tongue swiped the blood away, and I moaned at her taste. God, why did she taste so amazing? I pulled away, but she pressed her finger to my mouth.

"Suck," was all she said, and all the blood I did have left in my head rushed straight to my cock. *Fuck*, I knew I shouldn't do this, but it was so good. I sucked her finger gently. She was healing fast, but I wanted more. Though I knew I needed to stop before I lost control and took more than she was offering.

"Lexi, you trust me more than you should." I didn't trust myself most of the time, but this girl... This amazing, smart, and stubborn girl. I knew I was done for when I met her. I needed to slow the brakes on this a little.

"Go sit down. I'll warm up your breakfast, and if you still want to, I can take some blood from you." I'll be smart about it though, ration it out to a small amount every day. I didn't want to feel like I did this morning. Just that small amount already had me feeling a little better, and I would be able to feel her emotions again. It was a matter of safety that I could feel her. Well, that was what I was telling myself.

"Sounds good to me, and after, can you take me into Port Willow? I have some things I want to buy." The smile on her face as I told her yes made me happy. Did she think I would say no to spending alone time with her?

If she did, then she didn't know me, and today would change that.

SHE CHATTED AWAY as I set everything up. I'd done this many times before, but I didn't want to tell her that. Some things should be kept a secret.

"Why were you in the woods that night?"

I looked up from what I was doing, and her mouth quirked slightly as she glanced out the window. What was she talking about?

"I left you a note, and you didn't come, so I went to the woods to follow you."

My heart sank when I realized what she was talking about. She was in there because of me? I was in the woods watching her, then it became too much, so I went for a run to the cliffs to clear my head. When I heard her scream, I raced back. *Fuck*, it was because of me that it happened.

"I got your note, I just..." I let out a deep breath. I had to tell her the truth. "I was warned away from you. I was told I had to give you space with your new mates. So I was in the woods watching you, but I didn't know you saw me there. It's all my fault, Lexi. I should have gone to you earlier, but I was under orders to stay away."

And that was the truth. I wasn't to be near her while she established her bonds with her mates, especially with Ranger. Alaric had sent me on a mission to find out what she was, but it was also to keep me from her. He didn't like the connection we had, or how I felt for her. I was surprised I was still allowed to be around her yesterday. But then he needed me to compel Ada... There was always something I was doing for him, and that—compelling Ada— was something I didn't want to do.

This was so messed up. If I hadn't been kept

away, I might have known what Ranger was going to do. That he was breaking his bond with his pack-mate. That Callum would have been upset over this, and Lexi wouldn't have gone looking for me. Callum wouldn't have been there...waiting for her. Her face fell.

"Alaric?" was all she said. I nodded, but that was going to change. I wasn't going to do this anymore. I had been here working for long enough. I was quitting my job, and I would quit the pack too if that meant I could be with Lexi. I wouldn't put her in danger anymore. I was only here because Alaric's wife Laura had been murdered... by a vampire. I was here to protect everyone. But I failed the person who meant the most to me.

"I won't stay away, even if he orders it. I can't. You're mine, Lexi Turner."

I watched her smile grow into a huge grin.

"Always."

CHAPTER 15
LEXI

Galen said I was his. He literally said, "You're mine, Lexi Turner." It sent a warm feeling through my chest and straight to my core. I was glad, since there was no way I was giving him up after that kiss. God, why did it have to stop? I wanted to stay here all day kissing Galen, but then I also wanted to see Raff and Maverick and give them kisses. I hadn't seen them this morning.

The other surprise I got from Galen was an iPhone, right before we left his house in his old black car. Like, who just gives a person an iPhone? Apparently, Galen did, and he also had two cars and they were both black, which I didn't know. I thought he only had one. The only thing I really knew was they were classic cars, and one had four doors, while the other only two. This was the two door one, and it purred like a kitten. Okay that was a line I had heard from a movie. I had no idea what I was talking about.

I just couldn't get over Galen buying me a new iPhone. He told me it was a spare one he had just lying around doing nothing. Ah yeah right. It was the latest model and came out of a box that was still wrapped in plastic. I told him no, that my cell was fine, but then he asked me where I left my cell and I couldn't remember. On my bedside table when I checked the time this morning? But he had found it and set the new one up for me while I was eating a muffin at his house. I had so much food this morning I was going to pop. But it was a chocolate muffin, I couldn't say no to one.

He told me he could track the iPhone if I needed to be found, so it was for my safety. Which was the only reason I accepted it in the end. It felt amazing to be in his car, sitting next to him. We held hands as we drove to Port Willow, which I thought would be hard, since he was driving stick, but didn't affect him. I felt like I was almost driving it. When I asked if I could, the look he gave me was priceless. His cars must be like his babies, because I'd never seen that look on Galen's face. Instead, he offered to help me get my license. He'd teach me to drive, and could compel a license for me. I just laughed and shook my head. I wasn't going to cheat my way through life. That wasn't why I wanted to be with Galen.

As soon as we left the car, I made sure to act like

we weren't together. I didn't want him getting recognized with me and lose his job. He was a really good teacher. Plus, I didn't have long before I graduated. So it was only for a few months that we had to keep this a secret.

As we walked into Walmart, I saw a few people I recognized from school and some were shifters. I thought they were from Pack Rawlins, which seemed nicer than Pack Kenneally. I only remembered the tall, dark-haired one, Huxley Moore. He glanced our way when we stepped inside, but he turned back to his friend and paid us no attention. Galen stepped up beside me, and I tensed.

"It's safe here. Port Willow is neutral ground. There's nothing to worry about." I kept walking, watching Huxley. He turned to watch us move farther into the store, but he didn't say or do anything. He'd never spoken to me, sniffed me, or caused me issues at school. I thought that was why I remembered his name. If he hadn't been pointed out to me as a shifter by Maverick, I wouldn't have suspected he was one as he had a long scar down the side of his face, it went through the corner of his upper lip. For some reason I had thought shifters didn't have scars, but then Raff was covered in them. His tattoo's hiding all the evidence of what his uncles had done to him. Maverick had showed me all the shifters at school last week, said it was important for me to know them all, and there were more than I realized.

"RANGER IS IN A PANIC. Can you send him a message on the group chat?"

Apparently, there was a group chat, and since I now had a cell that supported these things, I was a part of it. The four of them had one for a few weeks now, but they'd failed to mention that. I was also somehow added into the "Lovell bros and Raff" group chat with all the brothers. Even Nash was in it, which made me not want to be in it. My new phone kept vibrating in my pocket, and I was starting to think I would never be alone again if they were always sending messages.

"Why did you add me to these chats then? Just tell him I'm busy." But Galen didn't listen, or he didn't care. He reached into my pocket in the middle of Walmart where anyone could see and handed me my phone. I groaned, and he laughed.

"Just say something. They're super excited that you have a phone that does more than make phone calls and basic text messages. And I know you barely did any of that to start with." I looked down at the screen and saw a bunch of messages, most of them from someone called 'Princess.' I opened the chat and saw Galen's message that we were just out shopping. Princess seemed a little worried...okay, a lot worried, asking where and when I would be back.

I laughed. "I'm guessing Princess is Ranger?" I could see the smirk on Galen's face. I laughed again and quickly typed out I would be back soon to watch the football game, then added 'your highness.'

My phone started going off, and it was better than watching a movie.

JETT: Hey, beautiful, I knew you couldn't resist wanting to be in my chat group.

Ranger: I was the one who added her, asshole.

Jett: But it was my group first. Scroll up, Lexi. See all the messages Ranger wrote about you before you let him near you. They're really good for a laugh.

Mav: Stop please.

Ranger: No, don't scroll up. Please don't, Lex.

Jett: I'm just fucking with you, Ranger. *Lexi, totally scroll up*

Nash: Will you stop. This is for important shit.

Jett: Never! This is too funny.

Jett changed his name to The better-looking brother.

I LOOKED over at Galen and saw he was laughing. See, this was why I didn't want one—I didn't want to see what Ranger had written about me. Okay, well, maybe I did a little. I was tempted to scroll up but instead, I quickly wrote back that I wouldn't, that I was busy shopping. Then I put it in my pocket again and tried my best to ignore it.

"I want to get some things for the pool. Josh is coming to swim this week, and I wanted to get some fun things we can use." Galen thought it was a great idea and helped me find where they kept all the pool stuff.

There was one of those blow up loungers, so I checked the price. It wasn't too bad, only twelve dollars. So I picked a yellow one, then I got a big blow up ball and some really cute goggles in red that had a snorkel attached that Josh could use to look in the water.

"Can you hold this while I go to the women's section and grab some new jeans?" I didn't even give Galen a chance to answer as I loaded his arms up and then walked toward the section that I remembered from my first real day here, when I came shopping with Jack and left him here. It was also the first day I met Nash, and I was surprised I was living in the same house as him and hadn't killed him yet.

I needed to replace the jeans that were damaged, but I also wanted to buy some nicer underwear. Maybe a matching lace set, something I wouldn't normally buy myself. On my way, I went past the pet section and noticed some colorful balls. I picked one up, and when I squeezed it, it squeaked. I laughed and took it with me. That would be fun to use later.

"PICK ANYTHING YOU WANT, and stop looking at the prices. I'm paying." I turned, my hand going to my chest.

"God, Galen. You scared me." I'd been in the women's section longer than I wanted to be. This wasn't like some shop with endless sexy underwear, but I didn't have enough for the set I really wanted. I'd have to put back the floating lounge chair, and I didn't want to do that.

"You're not paying. I have cash, and I intend to use it." The same eighty dollars that I'd come to Kiba with was in my sock, now ready to spend. I wasn't going to use his money or the money Alaric had given me. In the end, I decided to just grab a black lace thong and call it a day.

"Let's go get burgers after," I told Galen as I practically bounced to the check out. He just laughed, and that sexy grin came out. I liked this carefree, happy Galen. The day had only just started, but I could tell this was the start of a new life for me. Everything was feeling good, and I felt happy and whole.

I placed my things down, and the ball started to roll away. Galen picked it up, his brow quirked. I reached over and squeezed it, and his brows went up. I shrugged my shoulder.

"I just wanted to see if they play catch..." The devilish grin he made had me laughing so hard, that I had to hold onto him to keep upright.

"They aren't dogs...but I can't wait to see this, please throw it to Ranger first." He said, chuckling and shaking his head as he placed the ball back down and the lady took and scanned it. He placed his hand over mine that was still on his chest, and I smiled. This was nice, just a regular day out, shopping with a boyfriend...

"That will be seventy-three dollars and fourteen cents." She didn't sound like she was a fan of her job when she looked over at me, then to Galen. She had a sour look on her face, then she spoke.

"Mr. Donovani, I've been trying to set up a parent-teacher meeting with you at school, but now I'll have to call the school about what I have just seen here. This is very inappropriate."

Fuck.

CHAPTER 16

LEXI

Galen told me to go to the car and that he would take care of the check-out lady. I was worried, because if she saw us, then I guessed others did too. It wasn't much, since I just touched his chest. It was harmless flirting, but he wasn't as worried as I was. I knew he could compel people, but I didn't want him to have to do that every time we went out. He acted like nothing had happened when he got back to the car, so I pretended it didn't as well. He took my hand in his, and we went and grabbed some burgers.

I'd messaged Ada, asking if she was going to come over. The day was warming up so nice, and I didn't think I could handle all the testosterone that was going down outside the house. There had to be like thirty guys here. I assumed they were all pack members.

"I got you a chair and a cooler full of water and a few beers. They're for me, but you can have some if you want." Ranger was acting extra nice when I turned up. I wasn't too sure if he was worried that I'd read the messages, or if it was because everyone was staring at us...me.

"Thanks, I might have one when Ada gets here." I didn't know if I would even like beer, but I had a feeling I would relax and enjoy this game more if I had some alcohol in my system, which was something I didn't expect myself ever saying. But they were playing with one team in no shirts. There were all these sexy guys just flexing their muscles, and I was allowed to watch them all. Even Raff and Maverick out there playing...but they had shirts on. I needed Ada here now, but she wasn't coming for another hour. She would really appreciate this view, and she was missing out. Oh I know what would get her here faster. I took a photo and texted it too her. I watched the little dots dancing as she replied, "You are killing me."

"Can I join you?" Galen had a chair beside me and was already sitting. He smiled and winked at me before I even answered him. It had me curious.

"What are you up too?" He shook his head, still smiling.

"It's not as strong as yesterday, but I can sense your emotions. Your blood somehow connects me to you in a way I didn't think was possible. I know you're

126

looking at their bodies, getting yourself all worked up. I might be a little jealous... I don't have a body like that."

I COULD HEAR his thoughts again. When we arrived back, he went home and told me he was going to drink a small amount of my blood to test how much he needed since my finger didn't make a difference at all. That was all it took, and I was back to hearing him again.

"You shouldn't feel like that. Your body is perfect to me. Plus, I'm sure the guys would be feeling jealous too... I wasn't looking at *their* bodies." I laughed when I heard a low growl and saw everyone was now looking over at me. Ranger pointed to me, then to his eyes, and back to me. His lip quirked up in a playful way. I waved to him and blew a kiss. Maverick shook his head, smiling, and Raff surprised me when he blew me a kiss too. Some of the guys were getting restless at the game being stopped for this flirty fun, and they said so very clearly.

Someone was waving at me, I waved back. Then I realized it was Noah. Holy fuck... Chris Hemsworth had nothing on Noah's body. I knew he was huge... but shit, he was like... ripped.

"Noah wants to know when Ada will be here." I laughed. I couldn't hear him, but he knew Galen would and he seemed so okay with him, the other still seemed to avoid him.

"Maybe in an hour?" He was so adorable, and he was similar to Ranger. His heart was on his sleeve. But he was gentle and sweet, like Raff. Ada...just didn't see him that way. Well, that was what she kept telling me. I felt bad for him, since he was crushing hard on her. He was only like two years younger than she was. He was turning sixteen soon —he had told me many times—but she was already eighteen and leaving high school. I didn't know if it was the age thing she was hung up on, or if she wasn't attracted to him in that way. But he was just too sweet to have his heart broken. Even though Ada had made it clear many times she wasn't interested, he didn't listen. And I could see now that still wasn't getting through to him.

"Come on, let's see you play some ball," I yelled out. There were a few chuckles, then they returned to the game. I shrugged, maybe "play some ball" was a baseball thing or basketball? I had no idea, since I didn't really watch sports at all.

***

ABOUT TEN MINUTES LATER, there was a break in the game. The guys were all huddled together talking, although I didn't get why they would bother with game plans or whatever they were doing, if the other side could hear everything. Then there was some clapping and they all got ready to go again.

I never thought I'd be into football, but this was good. Maybe if they all didn't wear shirts... I watched as Noah started to run, but then slowed down and froze, looking behind me. Oh, was Ada here already? I swung my head around and saw an older woman. I was a little surprised. She was the first woman I had seen here before. She was wearing a lovely flower dress and had long blonde hair, but her face was red, her hands were wiping away tears, and I could see her body shaking. Oh god, she was sobbing.

There were two men beside her, and they were tall, like well over six feet to her smaller frame. I wondered if that's what I looked like next to the twins? They were holding her up, rubbing her back, and comforting her. They were followed by another two men who looked just as upset, and Nash was there behind them with his friend Elijah.

Oh fuck. That was Callum's parents. He had four dads, and that had to be them. I... *Fuck.* Alaric's punishment must have been bad. I looked over at Noah, shielding my eyes from the sun. He watched them as they walked towards the front gate. He looked pale, and the smile was long gone from his face.

"Noah," I called out to him. I'd forgotten. Oh god, how could I have been so stupid and forgotten that Callum was his big brother? He jogged over to me without question, Galen stood up and squeezed my shoulder as I stood to meet Noah.

"I am so sorry. I forgot Callum is your brother." He shrugged like it didn't matter, but you could see it did. If it didn't, then I would've been more worried about him, this was his brother. After seeing Noah and his parents, I realized this wasn't just punishing Callum, but his whole family. I stepped closer and wrapped my arms around Noah and gave him a big bear hug. He didn't react at first, but then his head lowered to mine and I could feel him physically sag into my hug, his arms loosely around my back, but I could feel his weight against me.

"Hey, don't get your scent on my girl." I pulled away to see Ranger, but I could see he wasn't being playful. He wasn't being rude either. I could see he was just as affected by what we all just saw. This was all so fucked up.

Raff came over with Maverick, and I moved into Ranger's arms. He looked terrible. I didn't know how to help him. What could I say?

"I'll go talk to Alaric, maybe I can get the punishment reduced..." Everyone looked at me like I was crazy. I glanced over to Raff, and he lowered his eyes. Even Maverick gave me a wry smile. Galen stroked my back a few times, but it was Noah who answered.

"No, his punishment is fair. It's just...you know. Hard."

Callum had hurt me, he'd hurt us all when he bit me, but I didn't want him to lose everything over something so stupid.

Because once you have good people, family that care about you. It would be stupid to throw it all away for a girl.

CHAPTER 17

LEXI

laric was in his office when I walked in. I didn't even knock, which was the reason for the look he was sporting right now. I wanted to smile at that, since Nash often wore that same expression... I could tell he wasn't happy to see me.

"Alexis," he ground out between his teeth. Yep, not happy at all.

"What is Callum's punishment?" I stood there with my hands on my hips, demanding he answer me. But I would be lying if I said he didn't sacred me...a little. He gave off a very intense vibe. He let out a huff of breath and stood up from behind his desk. He was tall, and the power I felt from him was strong.

"He is being exiled to Pack Bardoul. He is not to have contact with anyone in our pack. You will be safe here, Alexis. I have men patrolling the grounds at all hours of the day for any threats, or leaks that might have happened, and we will take care of you and keep you safe."

My mouth popped open. He was being exiled and couldn't speak to his pack? This was because of me. If I hadn't gone into the woods, if I hadn't told Ranger I wasn't interested in his packmate... Even though Callum was an arrogant asshole, this was too much.

"No, I don't think that's a very fair punishment. He can still call his family, right?" I could see Alaric didn't like the way I spoke to him, but I didn't give a shit. This was too much. Even prisoners got to call their families.

"This was hard choice. You don't understand pack rules, and he broke a very important rule. He is the first one to do this in almost fifty years. I did what was best for the pack." I went to argue, but Alaric beat me too it.

"You have a big heart, Alexis. I know this must look harsh to you, but there had to be consequences. He bit you, gave you his venom. If I didn't go hard on him, I would have a bunch of teenagers biting human females, so his punishment is also a warning to other pack members. Bardoul will educate him, and hopefully, he will learn from his mistakes.

"You must understand, when a shifter is exiled, it is never to another pack. Pack Bardoul has done this as a favor to Kiba. Callum is young and he needs a pack, as all shifters do. This is the best outcome for all involved. Now, if there is nothing more, please leave my office. I have a lot of work to do."

My mouth opened to protest, but I knew deep down inside it was true. If he let him get away with it, then there would be no stopping others from doing this if they knew they wouldn't be punished. And with how many women die during the transformation to shifter...there would be a huge death toll on Alaric's hands.

I didn't say anything, I just stormed out of his office. I felt like shit. Callum was Ranger's best friend, and just by being here, I had messed up so many lives already. I should have left when I had the chance, and everyone would've been better off. Except me, but I had done this long enough to know I could do it again. But now it was too late. I couldn't fix this by leaving now. What was done, was done.

I felt heavy in my chest, and I didn't want to go back out there and see the look on Noah and Ranger's face. When I rounded the corner, Raff was standing there. Was he waiting for me? I felt like a huge weight had been lifted off my chest at his open arms. I was near crying, and all of a sudden, everything just seemed to come crashing down.

I reached over to him, and he wrapped me in his arms without a word. I needed this. I'd missed him this morning, and even though I didn't want to admit it to myself earlier, I had needed him last night. As much as I was used to being alone, last night just felt like everything was too much all of a sudden. That I was being smothered, but that wasn't true. This was what it was like to have someone—a family, people who care and love you. I was that for Raff, and he was that for me.

I didn't want to sleep alone again...ever. And I didn't give a shit what Alaric had to say on that. If he had a problem, then I would move into Galen's place. I would still be on his property, safe within the walls, just not in the same white walls of the Lovell house. This house felt too bright, too clinical... everything about it was too much. Why the hell was this house so *fucking white*?

"Wanna go up to your room?" Raff asked, and I glanced up into his beautiful blue eyes. They were swimming with so much pain and worry. God, did I put those fears there? I shook my head.

"No. No, I can't stand these white walls any longer. Let's go back outside, but can you give me something before we go out there?" I gave him a playful smile, I wanted to see him happy again. I wanted the good start to the day not to be derailed by this shitty middle.

He didn't even have to think about it, he just nodded.

"I want a kiss..." I licked my lips as his hands snaked up to my cheeks. He leaned down slightly, nose brushing against mine before our lips touched.

So soft, so beautiful. It was gentle, like the first time we kissed, but it was also full of so much more. My toes curled as his tongue swept into my mouth, and when he ground his erection against my core, it went from innocent to so much faster. I moved against him, trying to get closer, needing everything he was giving me and not caring if anyone heard us.

When he pulled away slightly, our breathing was heavy between us. I couldn't stop my tongue from running over my lips, tasting him. He rested his forehead against mine, his eyes closed as he breathed me in.

"Sometimes, I worry you're not real. That this is all a dream, and tomorrow I'll wake up, back into the nightmare of my old life." My chest ached at his words. He had been through so much, yet he never fully opened up about it. This was special, he was giving me a little something. I hoped that one day, he would truly open up, know that I would never leave him. I was here forever and always.

After my runaway attempt, I knew I had a lot of work to do on that. I did abandon him, but only so he would be safe. He needed a pack and he couldn't be on the run with me, but I knew he would never have seen it that way.

I knew that was something I had to show him, since words like that meant nothing without the actions. I should know, that was how I had lived my whole life. His eyes slowly opened and looked right into mine. I felt them reach down deep inside, latching onto my heart, and I welcomed it.

"I love you, Rafferty," I whispered against his lips. There was a quiet moment where nothing was said, our chests breathing deeply, heavy with emotion.

"I love you, Lexi." I felt his body finally relax. The power I felt between us...it was there, stronger than ever. I needed him, all of him.

I pressed myself hard against his body, and my hands snaked up into his hair, tangling in the silver strands. I pulled him down as I took his mouth, showing him I was here, I was real, and that I loved him with every fiber in my body. His hands roamed my back to my ass, his fingers digging into my jeans as he pressed his erection into me again. I used that moment to pull myself up and into his arms, wrapping my legs around his waist. My core throbbed, needing the friction. The shorts he was wearing did nothing to conceal how turned on he was.

There was a loud crashing sound and laughter coming from the kitchen. We pulled apart slightly, a smile on my face. Fuck, that kiss was not for public display. I heard a chuckling sound coming closer, and I knew that laugh. The look on Raff's face told me he could see him, and he rolled his eyes in a playful way as his smile got bigger. Arms wrapped around me and Raff, and I felt the huge sweaty body behind me.

"Ranger..." I laughed as I tried to wiggle away from him, but he held on tighter.

"Gross, get your sweaty hands off me," Raff joked as he took a step back, but Ranger just held on, and I felt the deep rumble in his chest pressed against my back as he chuckled.

"That wasn't what you said last night," Ranger deadpanned back. My mouth dropped, did something happen between them last night? I turned to face Ranger. He took that opportunity to kiss me quickly before letting us both go and laughing.

"I was joking, but you smell amazing, Lexi. Do you want to maybe take this party somewhere a little *private*?" I rolled my eyes. He never stopped mentioning my smells, which I guess was something I had to get used to, living with shifters and vampires. Plus, I knew that I was turned on, very turned on.

Did I want to take this somewhere private?

Yes, I did. And not because I was giving off this scent and I didn't want all the pack to smell it too, but because I really did want to keep doing this. I wanted to go further and was tired of holding back, but Ada was on her way over. *Crap*.

"Maybe later. Ada will be here soon." Ranger just smirked, his brows raised, and I knew that face. He was up to trouble.

"All good. Noah will keep her entertained while Raff and I take care of you." His brows bounced up and down as he winked. I rolled my eyes and smiled. He was such a sexy dork at times. Ada was gonna hate me for this. I turned back to see what Raff wanted to do, and he gave my ass a squeeze. I could feel between my legs what he thought of the idea, and I let out a chuckle. I needed something...and this time, I didn't want to go to bed and take care of myself.

"Yes." It was almost a whisper, but the look on Ranger's face made me laugh. He wasn't expecting that answer. I dropped out of Raff's arms and took both their hands.

"Lead on to the private area, Ranger."

CHAPTER 18

LEXI

Well, the private area wasn't exactly private. It was outside, but on the other side of the house, farther away from where most the pack was getting the grill ready for a big cook out. That was what all the loud sounds were—they were in the kitchen getting ready.

There was a little alcove here, just hidden enough not to been seen. I was sure we would still be heard. But I was hoping there was enough noise out that it would be hard to really hear us.

"You have been such a tease today...coming out in these shorty shorts and showing off these legs to me. You have a sexy body, Lexi. You make me so hard every time I see you. But when you're rubbing yourself against Raff here, *fuck*. That is hot, and I want to join in so bad, touch you until you call out my name as you're on the edge of release..." A shiver went down my spine, and my heart started pounding hard in my chest. Fuck! Ranger's hand slid up my back and gathered some of the hair at the base of my neck. He tilted my head back, my mind swimming. Fuck yes, I wanted him to touch me, wanted to feel this. His mouth crashed onto mine, but only for a brief dizzying moment. "But...I want to watch too."

I let out a shuddering breath. *Oh fuck*. My thighs clenched together, needing the friction. I was so hot and worked up before he started talking. *He's talented at dirty talk.*

"Touch me," I demanded. He tilted my head back further, but his eyes looked above me as a grin crossed his face. He walked me backwards a few stumbling steps, then I felt the warmth of Raff behind me, his warm fingers skating under the fabric of my tank and along the waistband of my jean shorts. He pulled me in an almost possessive way to his warm, hard body, his hard cock barely contained in his shorts now resting against my ass.

Ranger used his hold on me to tilt my neck to the side, and Raff didn't waste any time. Using his tongue, he licked and nipped his way up my neck to my jaw. His hand followed up under my tank, resting just below my bra.

Ranger swallowed my moan with his lips as he pressed his body against mine. I was wedged between two hard bodies, and it felt amazing as Ranger's erection ground against my stomach. He was taller than me, so it wasn't hitting the right spot, but it didn't matter. Ranger's hand snaked down between us and popped the top button of my jeans. He pulled back slightly, watching my face for a moment, and I realized he was seeking permission. I nodded, I wanted this.

"Touch me, both of you."

My zipper lowered, then my shorts were loose, and I could now feel how wet I was. It surprised me when it was Raff who reached down and cupped my mound, rubbing his index finger against the wet spot on my underwear. I was all his firsts, and this was another first for him.

My body moved on his, seeking out his touch, needing the thin piece of fabric between us to be gone. I ground my ass back against him, causing him to let out a deep groan that sounded almost like a growl.

"You like that? You want more?" Ranger said, and my eyes opened and focused on him as his teeth dragged against his lower lip. His heated gaze flicked between my face and where Raff was touching me. Fuck, he was so devious. And he was *mine*.

I shoved my shorts down a little, giving Raff more room to move his hand. I reached out and grasped Ranger's cock through his shorts. He was hard and hot, and he grabbed my hand with a cocky smile, rubbed against it a few times, then took my mouth in searing kiss. Hands were roaming everywhere, and I reached back to rub against Raff's erection as his hand pushed under the cup of my bra and found my tight nipple. His pinching and rubbing it between his fingers had hot pleasure shooting down to my core, I was so wet now.

My underwear was shoved to the side. Fingers found my clit, and I let out a moan as my legs parted, wanting more. The heat of this moment was fueled by the lust and sexual tension that had been building between us all for weeks. It had finally bubbled up to the surface, and the reward was amazing.

A finger circled my clit, and I let out a whimper as another found my entrance. Two hands from two different men were working me. I needed them both to hold me up, my legs wanting to give out under the ecstasy I was feeling. Pleasure rocked through my system, and I saw stars. My head was pulled back, and Raff kissed me as I moaned, wanting more but also feeling too much, as I was so sensitive. I reached out to Ranger, trying to touch his cock... but he chuckled.

"This is about you, babe. Take it all. Use our hands to pleasure yourself. Don't worry about us, we'll get off just on you alone."

God, he was so unlike other guys. Most were takers, never givers, and here they both were, giving and not wanting anything in return. I rubbed my ass against Raff's erection harder, his body moving with mine. I knew he could come from this and I didn't need to touch him. I ran my hand down Ranger's chest and under his tee. His abs were like rocks, so tense, then I found his waistband. I tugged on the elastic a few times, and his chest rumbled deep.

"You don't have to ask. You can touch me anywhere, anytime."

I was so wet now, I could smell my own arousal in the air, and the guys were getting off on it as much as I was. I reached down into Ranger's shorts and found his hard, silky cock, throbbing and hot. I stroked a few times and rubbed my thumb over the head, swiping the pre-cum and circling it a few times. I smiled when the fingers working me from the inside stopped, which told me it was Raff that was strumming on my clit. Fuck, he knew what he was doing. He'd circle my clit and then give a few quick harder strokes that had my legs twitching, then slowly circle it again. He was teasing me, working me up to a mammoth orgasm, and I'd already had one...but I was greedy and wanted so many more.

"Don't stop," I panted to Ranger. I was so close, my chest heaving as a bead of sweat trickled between my breasts. His fingers sped up, curling and working my g-spot. Raff didn't let up on my clit until I gasped, called out their names, and really did see stars and the heavens as a huge orgasm rocked through me. My legs were unable to keep me standing, but they held me up as I rode that high.

There were a few kisses as Ranger pulled my hand from his cock, he hadn't come but he shook his head. "This was about you." He reminded me, he kissed my shoulder as my underwear was rearranged and my shorts were put back in place.

"Now that was hot." Ranger smirked as he licked his fingers, the same ones that had been inside me. He winked and took my hand. I looked down to see how Raff had gone, he had a darker patch on the front of his shorts. I smiled, I did that.

Raff spoke up as he took my other hand. "Ada has arrived. I'm just gonna quickly change." He kissed me and ran off in the opposite direction.

I had no idea how I was going to walk back out there and not look like a chick who just got off... twice behind the house. But these were my boyfriends. My mates.

No one would say anything and make it awkward...right?

CHAPTER 19
MAVERICK

I was drowning in guilt and memories. My wolf was out of sync with me for the first time in my life and... Just... *Fuck*. Watching Lexi dying, then Galen. All that blood...so much blood on white floors, white rugs. So much red.

It brought up memories of my mother's death and the reason why our house was white—because dark rooms hide dark men. Shadows are easier to see on a white wall than a dark one. My mother, lying on the floor of the living room... I didn't see her, but I smelled the blood. I could taste it in the air.

After that, Father had the whole house painted white. He said if it had been that way before, maybe my mother could have been saved. But we knew it wouldn't have stopped them. Vampires my father pissed off had come to send him a warning, and that was the first one. *My mother.* He said he'd killed the assholes who did it, and that was right before Galen moved in.

My heart was pounding in my chest. So much bad shit has happened, but now I wasn't sure. How could I give my heart to someone, knowing that something could come and take them from me? Like they did my mother.

I didn't know what to do, and I felt uncomfortable around Galen, so much so that I hadn't spoken to him. I was pretty much avoiding Lexi, because I felt like my heart would break into a thousand pieces. *Fuck.* I didn't know what I was doing and this wasn't like me.

I ran my hands through my hair and looked up. Most of the guys had gone in to grab meat and stuff for the grill, while the other half waited out here. I wasn't as close to them as Ranger was. Saint was my best friend, and I preferred to keep my friends' group small.

I watched the way the pack was avoiding Galen. I could see he was trying so hard to just fit in, that he wanted to fit in now more than ever. When he sat beside Lexi, I thought this was huge. She accepted him as he was, and even though I could hear some of the pack muttering shit under their breath, Galen didn't let on, didn't flinch or frown. He just smiled and spoke to her, like this was a normal day here in Kiba and we were all one big happy family. It was the opposite. Everyone here was fucked up in one way or another.

But Galen, he just kept making her smile. He acted like he was always a part of this, being out here watching the guys play football. It just showed he was better for her then half of these assholes who still wanted to compete for her. I knew of two who had spoken to my father earlier, telling him that she was their mates. It just made me angry because I knew they wouldn't accept Galen and that was wrong. So, so wrong.

They would never have her, she wouldn't want them, especially if they thought it was funny to put him down. They were jealous, and the more Galen ignored them, the more they whispered shit. I was so fucking angry that I tackled Asher harder than I normally would.

When he picked himself up, he spat on the ground at my feet and growled, "Vamp lover."

I guess not everyone was so accepting of our family pack with Lexi being a mixed one. I had heard of shifters from other packs joining new ones to be with their mate. It didn't happen often, but it was good to have fresh blood in the mix.

This was definitely a first for us here. My father was pretending to be okay with it all, but I knew better. He didn't want Lexi to pick Galen, at all. I wasn't sure if it was the mixed thing and being two of his sons were part of it, or a safety thing. Like he was scared Galen might attack us. That would never happen. But my father had sent him away last week, trying to force space between them both. It didn't work though.

To make matters worse, my feelings for Galen were out in the open—at least to everyone that had witnessed me and Galen while he was dying. My father hadn't spoken to me, but I didn't care. He was an asshole alpha first, and a shitty father second.

Fuck. Everything was fucked up.

I WALKED OVER TO NOAH, since he was better than any of the others here to talk to, plus he was really accepting of Galen and I liked that about him. The reason I was seeking out Noah was I just couldn't bring myself to sit down beside Galen now that he was alone. I didn't know what to say to him, and I didn't want anyone knowing our business.

"Hey," I called over to Noah. He was stretching, getting ready for another game.

I did enjoy playing football. We couldn't actually play for any human teams after our first shift, but basketball was okay as long as it was mix of humans and shifters, since it wasn't a contact sport. Well... not in the same sense. So, this was the next best thing—all the teens in the pack getting together and playing.

The younger guys played over at Luca Brooks' place. Luca, I thought, was Noah's best friend, maybe his packmate? They were the same age and I'd seen them hang out together, but Noah was too big to play with the younger guys. He was bigger than me. Fuck, he was bigger than most of us here, including his older brothers.

The part I liked the best on these days was we always went for a run after. It was like a spring break tradition around here, always has been. We did this every day for spring break, and on the last day, we had a huge party and invited the girls around so the guys could find their ideal mates. The dating pool was very limited around here, which was why so many of us were single. Well not me anymore.

"Ready for me to kick your ass again, Mav?" Noah teased as he shoved my shoulder playfully, making me stumble back a little, but I smiled. The guy was built like a house. He was tall and good looking, so I could see why the girls at school looked at him the way they did. He was like a Viking god, blond with striking blue eyes, but with the attitude of a playful panda—big, soft, and cuddly.

"You might be bigger, but I can out run you!" I

punched his shoulder back, but he didn't move, and I smiled to myself at that. He grinned as I heard a car approaching, which must have been Ada. I could hear my brother and Raff taking care of Lexi—*real good* care. I rolled my eyes and tried to block them out, but I was sure everyone here was listening, saving this up for spank bank material later. That didn't sit right with me... They shouldn't be listening to something between mates.

"Maybe on two legs, but on four, I smash you." I looked up at Noah and shook my head of my dark thoughts. I needed to stop where my mind was going and focus on this. I let out a deep breath and I smiled at Noah because it was true, he was fast in huge wolf form.

The thought had my wolf stirring to run now. He was all out of sorts and hadn't been the same since the attack. I didn't know how long he was going to be like this, so restless. I couldn't control him. It was like that night opened up more of the animal within me, the one that I'd held back for so long.

I looked back to see Galen had left, and I guessed he was letting Ada in.

"I think my girl is here, wish me luck." Noah's huge grin made me realize I was destroying everything with Lexi and Galen by getting lost in dark thoughts. And here Noah was, not caring that Ada had told him there wasn't a chance they would be more than friends. That grin and the way he bounced away into a jog showed that he would do anything to convince her they could be more.

I'd had that... Days ago, I'd had all that, and now I was all messed up and fucking up the one good thing I did have, because fear overrode it all.

Fear was a powerful feeling.

CHAPTER 20
LEXI

W hen I got back to my chair, everyone was looking at us and smiling knowingly, which pissed me off. Like come on, at least pretend you weren't listening.

"Hey, ignore them. They're just jealous because I have the hottest mate and all they have is their hands," Ranger said, that last bit a little louder than the rest. Yeah, like they would miss that. They could hear us from space if they wanted to, and they obviously wanted to hear. I admit, we weren't somewhere super private, but still, regular people with normal hearing wouldn't have heard us. They could pretend they didn't listen, instead of smiling and nodding at us. I let out a deep breath, since there was no point being upset over a bunch of dicks.

"I hope you filled your spank banks, because it'll be a long time before anyone wants to touch your

—" Ranger's hand covered my mouth and stopped me from finishing the rest. He laughed, and I couldn't help the smile that spread under his hand. He let go, taking my arm, he swung me around to face him. I let a small gasp leave my lips. He grinned as I let him pull me down with him into the sunchair I was in earlier. I kicked my feet off to one side as he held me in an almost cradle, and he wrapped his arms around me and kissed my temple. I let out a giggle when I saw the guys now looking everywhere but us. I guessed I made them feel awkward, but it was nice to turn the tables. I snuggled against his body. He was so warm, and even though it was nice out, there was a slight chill in the air when the wind blew.

"You're fucking hot and a badass," Ranger said, and I just smiled into his chest and took a deep breath of his scent.

That had me thinking... If they could smell that I was their mate, was that why they smelled so good to me? The whole scent thing was still something I was going to take a while to really be okay with, but it had me thinking about how they all smelled like something different to me. Even if they wore after-shave, I could tell who it was by their scent. Was this a new thing? No, it wasn't like me warming up Galen's arm, or having his thoughts in my head. The guys all had scents that attracted me to them from the start.

Wildflowers. Which suited Ranger... He was a little wild but totally pretty. *And he knew it*. Same went for Raff, Mav, and Galen. They all had the most wonderful scents. But then, I had picked up the scents of some of the others in the pack, and some weren't that bad. Like Jett and Lyell. I still wasn't happy with Lyell, so his scent wasn't as good now. I guess that made them who they were. They were all different.

But if I could smell others...did that mean they were my mates? Oh fuck, I hoped not. I felt Ranger rub my arm tenderly, and I gazed up at him, his brow pinched in the middle and a brow raised in question. I just gave him a smile and shook my head. No, I had no time for anyone else, so they better not have been my mates. Fuck, I barely have time for the ones I have.

"Where is Mav? I haven't really seen him at all." I looked around and still couldn't see him. He'd been out here playing football earlier, so maybe he was at the grill. Ranger just shrugged and held me closer to his chest.

"No idea. It just means I get you to myself a little longer." I closed my eyes and listened to his heart-beat. It was solid and steady. I felt relaxed and safe in his big arms.

"Hey, sexy lovers," a happy and cheerful female voice sang out, and I smiled.

I opened my eyes, and the sun was a little bright

at first, but I laughed. I watched Noah gesturing to the chair beside me, which Galen had used earlier. Ada was here, and I was so happy to see her. I needed someone who didn't have a dick to hang out with.

"Girls talk. Go do your football things now," Ada said to Noah as she actively avoided him, shooing him with her hand, but he didn't care. He just smiled with his hand on the back of the chair. She rolled her eyes at me, but the hint of a smirk was there. I tried to hide my smile, but she saw it.

"Stop it." She smacked my arm teasingly.

"Hey, don't be hitting my woman... Noah, your girl here is feisty." Ranger was in a shit stirring mood. I could feel the rumble of his laugh under my body as Ada shot the deadliest glare at him.

"I like them feisty," Noah replied and chuckled. It was making Ada bright red, and I didn't know if that was from blushing or if she was mad.

"Alright, time for you guys to go. Girl talk time." I tried to pull away from Ranger, and he reluctantly let me go. He made a sad sound when I made him get up, and he pouted at me. I reached up and grabbed his chin, pulling him down to eye level. When he was close enough, I put both my hands on his cheeks and squished his face until his lips looked like a fish.

"Be a good boy, and I'll give you a kiss and maybe something a little later." I could see one of his brows rise. I quickly kissed him and let go, giving him a little shove to get him moving, but his smile was huge.

"I hope it's a little of what we did before, and not this morning." He winked, and I laughed. I forgot I teased him earlier. Noah still didn't get the memo, and I watched as Ranger smiled and shook his head. He wrapped his arm around Noah's back and moved him away from us. Noah was very reluctant to go, but Ranger said something to him and it was enough to make him jog away.

Ada looked at me, her eyes huge and saying to me *"Oh my god, what the hell?"* very clearly. So I rolled my eyes and smiled, which meant *"I know right? Boys."*

I didn't realize girls had so many ways to talk without saying a word. Well, not until I got myself a best friend in Ada, because that was what she was—a best friend. My very first.

"It kinda sucks we can't actually *chat* chat, if you know what I mean." I slumped back into the chair and held my hand out to her. She took it and squeezed.

"I know. I was worried about coming back here today. And then you weren't at the gate and..." I could tell she was biting her tongue from saying Noah. I laughed, but she didn't.

"I'm sorry, I was a little busy..." Her mouth popped open, and I nodded. She leaned in, and I held up two fingers. Her mouth dropped more, but I didn't say anything else. We had more eyes on us now, and they weren't for me. They seemed to be directed at Ada.

She looked out to where I was looking at them all. They were setting up another game...but now, no one was wearing a shirt. I wondered if it was for Ada, since I was told they normally didn't have girls here while they played, at all. I guessed it would be hard to explain how they were playing full contact without any gear on, when they all got up and walked away with barely a scratch. Plus, she knew what they were, which would make dating someone a little easier on them. So I guessed they were maybe a little more interested in getting to know Ada.

My almost dying gave Ada the best buffet of men —the very sexy but some totally asshole shifters. Well, she did say she would like to have a boyfriend or two, right? I was sure she said two. Her dream guys could be out there. I was sure there were many packmates looking for someone special, and here she was.

"Would you like a drink, Ada?" She gasped at the voice that came from behind us, and I turned to see it was Saint. Now her face really did look a shade of crimson, and I held my hand to my mouth to stop myself from laughing. She so had a crush, bad!

"No, thanks," she squeaked out as he just stood there, staring at the back of her head before glancing over to me. Saint cocked his head and grinned as he stepped in front of us. He stopped right in front of Ada and pulled his T-shirt off, throwing it onto Ada's lap. She caught it, and he winked. Her eyes widened, and her mouth dropped open, obviously lost for words. That even surprised Saint.

"Hold that for me. I'll come back for it later." She just nodded, and that sexy grin was back on his face. He turned and headed to the guys, strutting away. I could see it, everyone could and a few pushed him and let out a few growls.

"Ah, guess there are a lot more peacocks here in Kiba than I first thought." Galen announced as he appeared beside me and squatted beside my chair. I couldn't help but laugh at his statement. I glanced at him, my hand moving without thinking, and I couldn't stop myself from running my fingers through his hair dark curls. His eyes darkened slightly at my touch, but he leaned into my hand as I brushed it over the stubble on his chin.

"Oh, don't say that. It might encourage them all to start strutting around, showing their muscles." I replied, but I didn't really mind that too much.

Ada made a sound, so I turned to see her holding Saint's top up close to her face, peeking over at the guys in front of us.

And yep, my big mouth. We were both looking at the group of guys, literally strutting. They looked like over exaggerated models on a catwalk, their arms flexing and giving us a "gun show."

Even Ranger was out there, and when he saw me watching, he kissed his biceps and pointed at me with the biggest grin on his face.

"These are all for you, babe!" he called out, and I shook my head, laughing.

Yep...bunch of peacocks.

CHAPTER 21
LEXI

"So what did you think, Lex?" I looked up at Ranger as he approached me, but from the corner of my eye, I saw Maverick standing just off to the side. I felt like there was something going on with Maverick, since he'd really avoided me today. I wasn't sure if he was upset with me, or if it was a Maverick thing.

I stood up and reached my hand out to Maverick, I smiled when he walked over to me and took it. As soon as his fingers were laced with mine, I felt like I could relax. There was something going on, but I didn't know what it was yet. I was just glad he was still here with me.

"About what?" I asked. Raff laughed with Maverick, and Ranger just shook his head and kissed me.

"I told you she wasn't watching you," Raff said, and I turned and slapped him playfully.

"Shhh...that's a secret. I watch all my boyfriends... Some more than others," I teased Ranger. He moved towards me, taking my cheeks between his big hands and kissing me quickly.

"Lies, all lies, Lex, and you know it. You watch me the whole time. But because I know you're hungry—you're always *hungry*—I'm gonna get you a burger and then you're gonna give me my 'something later.'"

He stepped back, winking at me, and I could feel the warmth in my body starting to burn hotter. Before I could answer Ranger, Raff moved in, taking his place, and kissed me, his tongue playing over my lip before he moved away. *Wow.*

"You girls want a drink? Water?" Raff offered us, and I smiled so big. He didn't talk much in front of Ada, and he'd asked her if she wanted a drink. My heart wanted to burst.

"Yeah, water...some vodka would be better," she mumbled, and I nodded.

"Yeah, both sounds good to me," I told Raff, and he ran off. Maverick tried to let go of my hand, but I wasn't having it. He was looking at his feet, and I just wanted to fix this.

"Did I do something?" His eyes flicked up to mine, the color swirling like he was struggling not to shift right now. He didn't say anything, but he squeezed my hand a little tighter. I wished he would talk to me.

"You need to go for a run?" I didn't know what was happening between us right now. I was getting such mixed signals. His eyes focused on me, the color now the beautiful dark green they were normally, then he shook his head and looked down to his feet.

Reaching up, I cupped his jaw and moved his face close to mine. I gently kissed his soft lips, and he kissed me back. He took hold of my waist, and I knew he needed something from me. If it was quiet cuddles, then that's what I would give him. I turned him and pushed him into the chair.

He let out a "*humf*," and I giggled. Ada was trying not to watch us, and I could see her shift slightly when a big figure walked over and blocked out what was left of the sun.

I used that moment to straddle Maverick against the chair. His hands came straight to my ass and held on tightly, so I took that as a good sign.

"We good?" He closed his eyes and rested his forehead on mine, then took a few deeps breaths. I was so lost and had no idea what was upsetting him so much. He wasn't giving me any answers, but when his head pulled away, he nodded.

"Just had shit on my mind, it's not you. I'm just... just overthinking shit." He moved in and kissed me. When his tongue licked the seam of my lips, all the noise and people at the party disappeared. It was just the two of us. My hands on the back of his neck pulled him closer, wanting his body against mine.

"Get a room," I heard someone's voice call out, breaking through my bubble with Maverick, but I didn't want to pull away. I was so worked up, I bet I smelled like a bitch in heat, and I could tell Maverick was just as worked up as me. He pulled my hips down and let me feel how worked up he was. *Better slow this down.* I spun on Maverick, so I was now sitting in his lap, my back to his front and now facing Noah, who was taking off his shorts? *What the hell?*

I put my hand up to block the sight. I looked over to Ada, and she was staring at Noah. Like really staring at him. I saw her tongue dash out quickly, wetting her bottom lip. I shook my head and, with my hand positioned just right, I looked back over at Noah.

"Ah, what the fuck are you doing, Noah?" Maverick asked. Noah cocked his head to Ada and smiled.

"Ada wanted to see a wolf, so I told her I would shift for her." My other hand went to my mouth to cover the laughter I knew would spill out if I didn't hold on. Ada must have seen me move and gently pushed my shoulder. The giggles came out, right as Noah went from human to wolf. By the sound Ada made, she was either excited that he shifted for her or that she was seeing a wolf shifter, I wasn't sure. She really had mixed feelings for him.

"Wow. Holy shit. He really is a wolf." I could feel Maverick laughing under me, and my heart wanted to burst. He always seemed too serious, and it was nice for him to let go. I turned and laughed with him. I kissed him a few times before I turned back and saw Ada leaning over and stroking the huge wolf in front of her.

"He is so soft, like holy crap. Do you get someone to brush your fur?" My mouth dropped, and I could see Saint standing nearby, just watching Ada. Then I realized there was a lot of guys watching her pet Noah. *Oh fuck, she was petting Noah.*

"Ada, stop. Fuck, petting him is like, you know, making out for them. You only stroke your mate." Well, that's what Raff had told me. Her hand jerked away like Noah was on fire, and she held her hand to her chest like she had been burned.

"He told me I could pet him. He didn't say anything." That had Saint over here in a flash, and he growled low at Noah. At first, Noah didn't move, but a second warning from Saint had him moving quickly but not far from us.

Ada was totally freaking out, and I felt terrible that I didn't warn her about it. I was distracted and didn't think twice. But I guessed I thought Noah would be a good guy and tell her at least. Then again, this was Noah. He was crazy about her, so I should've known he would trick her into something.

"It's okay, Ada. He should've told you," Saint said, trying to calm down Ada. He growled low again, and I watched as Noah's ears pinned back slightly as he crouched low. Was Saint like an alpha to him, or were they getting ready to fight? I groaned and rubbed my hands down my face. I didn't want to see any fighting, since I was having a good time again.

Then I had an idea. I leaned over and grabbed the bag full of pool goodies that I'd left near my chair, reaching in and grabbing the ball I'd bought earlier. I couldn't help the grin now spread across my face as I handed it to Ada. She looked down at it, and I could see her brow furrow, when she squeezed it her eyes lit up when she knew what I'd just given her.

"You wanna play catch?" She waved the ball at Noah's face, and there was a bunch of chuckles from around us. Noah perked up and shuffled closer, but he was really avoiding Saint. She threw the ball, not very far, but he got up and chased it.

We all laughed, and my tummy hurt from laughing so much when he brought it back and dropped it at her feet, sitting with his tongue lolled to the side. She laughed and picked it up, but this time, she stood up and threw it further before he chased it.

"I think someone is trying to get back in the good books," Galen said, and I looked up as he handed me a plate with a burger and then held out another one. Maverick hesitated at first, but then took it from him.

"So, I heard from a certain Alpha, that it was someone's birthday yesterday and they didn't tell us. And in the crazy shit day we all had, we all forgot." Galen said as he winked at me. I looked around, since it wasn't mine. Ranger and Raff came back, holding two glasses and a few bottles of water under their armpits. Raff had three plates in his hands, and he leaned over and gave one to Ada. It made me so happy that they didn't forget about her. Then everyone took a seat on the grass around us.

"Raff, you should have told us sooner, this was huge. I'm so sorry we all missed it" Galen said. I stopped mid bite and looked at Raff. He just shrugged and mumbled it wasn't a big deal. Oh my god, how could I have missed something so important? My heart sank for him. I didn't wake up with him, I...

"Raff, why didn't you tell me?" My eyes were starting to water, and my throat got tight. I didn't even share my bed with him, he woke up alone on his eighteenth birthday and no one wished him a happy birthday all day.

He didn't meet my eyes, but he shrugged and shoved the burger in his mouth. I knew then that he hadn't ever celebrated a birthday before, not like the others. His birthdays were more like mine...alone. I'd never had a birthday party or a birthday cake, and presents were something I only dreamed about.

I stood, Galen taking my plate as I wrapped my arms around Raff's back. "Happy birthday, I whispered as I tried hard to keep the tears in, but a lonely one escaped, rolling down my cheek and onto his tee.

"It's okay. There was more important things happening. No big deal." His hands were on mine as he held me to him. I felt his heart racing, and I couldn't believe I didn't know.

"Raff. It is a big deal. We want to make it special, throw a huge party, man. You turned eighteen, and you didn't tell us." Ranger told him.

I turned to the others and said, "You better tell me your birthdays. I'm never going to miss another one." I was going to make sure Raff had the best late birthday ever.

CHAPTER 22
LEXI

Burgers were the best, and the ones the guys had all cooked up were amazing. I'd stuffed my face. Now the stars were out, and the music was perfect and not too loud. Raff had gone inside to change again he had said, but I knew he just needed time alone for a moment. I thought he was a little overwhelmed by Ranger's party plans, and he had *plans*. I thought my plan was a little better, since I was hoping we could go out to dinner, maybe somewhere in Port Willow. I'd seen some restaurants around there, and it would be nice. Just the five of us. But have a special one on one lunch with him. Alone, together.

"Let's have something to drink." Ada snapped me out of my thoughts as she reached over and took her glass. It was full of clear liquid, and I was told it was vodka and Sprite. I took mine as I shuffled my ass on Maverick. I'd jumped back onto his lap when Raff left, and I hadn't let him up. He wasn't getting away from me. I took a small sip, and I could taste the alcohol instantly. I thought vodka didn't like have huge a taste, but it was strong. Ada's eyes flared open to me as she coughed.

"Who mixed this? It's like vodka with a dash of Sprite." She asked. Maverick pulled my wrist holding onto the glass towards him and took a sip. He shook his head and laughed.

"Ranger is trying to get you drunk, I think. That's strong." More laughter came when Ranger shook his head and pointed to Galen, who looked... guilty?

"I didn't make them." Ranger smiled, Galen was over to us fast, taking the glasses from our hands and making the liquid slosh over the sides in his haste.

"I'm so sorry. I don't mix mine, so I didn't know... I've never made one before. I should've asked how you liked them."

I snatched mine back, and so did Ada.

"It's fine, just means I won't need more than one to feel a little buzzed." Ada smiled and took a huge mouthful, but the grimace on her face made me decide to sip it.

Galen was watching me closely. The group around us had grown and I'd noticed that quite a few guys were sitting closer to Ada, but most looked as if they were trying to avoid being close to Galen. It upset me a little, but Ranger sat right down on the grass with him earlier, shoulder to shoulder, not caring about the stares. Galen acted like he didn't care either, but I knew he still would. It still upset me that he was excluded here, even more so than Raff was, and Galen had been here for six years. I took this as a good time to show them all, all the shifters of Kiba, that Galen wasn't going anywhere.

"Hold this for me?" I spun and gave Maverick the glass. He kissed my shoulder as I turned in his lap. I leaned forward to where Galen was still standing in front of me and grabbed onto the long-sleeved shirt he was wearing. His eyes followed my hands as I pulled him in so close our noses were touching.

I could hear the gasps and silence around, then the music the only thing I heard as I moved in and took his lips with mine. His hand sneaked up into my hair, and he pulled me closer, which caused my back to arch in Maverick's lap, my ass pressing harder into his now hard cock. With one hand, Maverick held me against him, grinding against my ass as I pressed hard back against him. Maverick moaned the same time I did, and Galen swallowed it with a hungry kiss.

When Galen pulled away, I licked my bottom lip before I leaned back onto Maverick. I reached up and moved his face closer to mine. He didn't need to be asked, he just took my mouth. He was just as hungry as Galen, like he was trying to taste him on my lips. Tongues and teeth, this was wild coming from Maverick, and I fucking loved it. It was Ada who broke the silence.

"Okay, you really do need to get a room." I pulled away, my lips tingling, and I was so worked up again. I thought a room sounded good just about now, but also, maybe a little too much.

"Well, I guess there's no more wondering if Galen is in or out... I take it that was your way to tell us that you have taken him as a mate, Lex."

I eyed Ranger and looked over to Raff, then gave them a lazy smile as I took the cup back from Maverick and drank the whole glass of vodka. It burned as it went down, the taste yuck, and I shook my head, trying to get the taste away.

"He's always been in. He just didn't know it."

I could hear a lot of talking, but I blocked it out as Galen took my hand. I felt two more hands and looked down to see all my mates were touching me. In that moment, something clicked into place.

This was right, this was me giving my heart away to four guys. For the first time in my life, I felt protected, loved, worshipped, and happy. I never wanted this feeling to end, and I would do anything to keep this.

I looked up to the sky. It was cloudy, but there was a small break that allowed me to see the stars.

They were so far away, but they were always there when I looked up. Then I saw a streak of light.

"Shooting star, Lexi. Make a wish," Galen said as he kissed my palm.

"I wish upon a star..." I thought that's how it went. I wished that this would never end. That this was forever, and nothing would hurt us now that we'd all found each other.

But something deep inside told me that something was coming.

And I needed to be ready.

CHAPTER 23

LEXI

I felt hands on my body, a lot more than two, and I realized I was waking up to more than just Raff today. I kept my eyes closed and smiled as hands roamed under my sleep shirt and up to my nipples. I pressed into them, my breathing getting deeper, and I could feel myself getting wet. *Fuck, I'm always wet around them.*

I felt kissing on my neck as someone took my mouth. His tongue wasted no time, meeting mine with a deep hunger. I ran my hands down the closest body to me, along his bare chest and to the waistband of his boxers. God, they were tight as I dipped the tip of my index finger beneath the band and tugged lightly. He growled, and I opened my eyes to see it was Ranger. He took my wrist and pressed it over his hard cock. It wanted to break him free from that thin material holding him tight. I was kissing Maverick, and I bit his lip as his twin rubbed himself against my palm. This was so...dirty.

I felt a hand snake around my thigh, my legs opening, giving more room to where I wanted to be touched the most. I glanced down to see it was Galen. I wanted to get off so bad, I needed this. It felt like forever that we'd all been toying with each other, pushing and pulling. The large warm hand of Raff pressed between my legs, cupping me and starting to rub against my core, my hips chasing after the pressure every time it moved away from my clit. I moaned out their names.

I wanted to touch Ranger, see Raff come, take Galen, and see how far I could push Maverick. *All of them.*

"Lexi..."

I moaned again, but the hands felt strange now. Why was the bed shaking? Was this an earthquake?

"Lexi, you're having a dream," I heard louder, the image in front of me changing as I opened my eyes.

I looked up into Raff's face. He looked so cute and sleepy, with his hair all messed up and those eyes.

"How are you like, so hot?" I asked. His brows went up, and he threw his head back and chuckled.

"Yeah, I think our mate here was having a very

nice dream," Ranger said, and I turned to see him looking just as disheveled as Raff. *What the hell?*

I sat up, rubbing my hand over my face. I was in my room, in my bed, with Ranger, Raff... I looked down and saw Maverick was also here. His eyes were closed, but I could tell he was awake. But... "Where is Galen?"

"I'm here. Apparently, my scent makes it hard for the guys to sleep, so I tried to stay away."

I heard Maverick make a groaning sound at that. I looked over to Ranger, and he rolled his eyes.

"I said that it was messing with my senses and my body couldn't relax. I did say to come back when I passed out, not to stay over there all night. I can still smell you anyway, so I guess it's just something I'll get used too. I didn't really think about it when we all agreed to sleep in here."

I threw myself back down on the pillow, then I felt the bed dip.

"So, you have a nice dream, Lexi?" Galen asked.

"Stop smelling me, assholes. And don't wake me up when I'm just getting to the good bit in the dream. I was just about to have sex with...*Zac Efron*." I could hear them all groan.

"You know, you can lie all you want...but it wasn't Zac you were calling out for," Ranger teased. I just shook my head at him. Okay, I was caught having a good dream...a really hot and heavy, *I need to recreate this in real life* kind of dream. Instead, I rolled over and cuddled into Raff. Last night, I decided that today was going to be his birthday do over day. Everyone agreed while he was inside, so today was going to be all about Rafferty King.

"Happy eighteenth Birthday, Raff." I moved in and kissed him.

CHAPTER 24
RAFFERTY

I'd been feeling strange since I woke up, especially since I didn't get the best night's sleep. I hadn't wanted to mention to Galen last night that it was his scent that wouldn't let my wolf relax too, and even while he was in the closet, his scent was enough to have my skin prickle. My wolf was on alert all night, even though I knew he wouldn't hurt us. I took a deep breath and tried to settle into Lexi, but I felt exhausted.

Lexi was well rested, and if anything, she seemed happier than ever waking up next to the three of us. I could smell her worry when she didn't see Galen at first, and the happiness I saw wash through her at knowing he was there made me feel bad for wanting to ask him to sleep in another room tonight.

Like Ranger had said, I'd have to get used to it

now that Lexi had let him in. I felt better knowing that she had accepted him, and it felt like we were complete now with him. A real family, a pack of our own.

I still couldn't believe the way my life had changed in just a month. If Keene hadn't picked me up running my uncle's shit, if I didn't finally let Shelly convince me to go here to Kiba...I would probably be dead, and that was the best scenario.

"I'm taking you to a birthday lunch, so go get ready but keep the sexy bed hair," Lexi said, running her fingers though my hair a few more times. My wolf wanted to be stroked by her, and I could feel him wanting to nuzzle her. "We're going out, so get moving." I laughed when I realized that I was nuzzling her.

My wolf had grown so strong, it would be hard to contain him now. He wanted to claim Lexi and for Lexi to claim him. To bond. That was something that would never happen, but I was still so happy without it. I never wanted her to become a shifter, and now we knew that couldn't happen. Whatever Lexi was, she was perfect, and she called to my wolf like no other ever had. Nothing would change how I felt about her.

She pulled away from me and clapped her hands.

"Okay, boys, time to get out. I'm taking a shower." I felt the bed jostle and looked up to see Ranger wearing nothing but boxers, strutting his way to Lexi's bathroom.

"Hey, what do you think you're doing?" Lexi called out to him, her head cocked to the side when he turned back to us with that shit eating grin.

"I need to shower too, so I thought we could save time. I wash your back, you wash my—" A pillow hit him before he could finish. As I had come to know Ranger, I knew he wasn't going to finish with, "wash my back." And Mav knew it too.

It was Galen who had us all moving, but I didn't need too much pushing to go get ready. Lexi and I were going out, *alone*. I would have her most the day to myself, something I had wanted to have for a while now.

I WAS NERVOUS, but I didn't know why. I had thought Lexi would want to go to Port Willow, maybe eat down there, but instead, she asked to go to Port Angeles. Everyone said it was fine, that we were Pack Kiba, and if there was a problem with any packs down there, to call and they would come. There were truces with other packs. They told us to have fun and relax, but that was hard to do when you were alone in a car with the love of your life.

"What kind of food do you like?" she asked, her bare feet on the dashboard, and I smiled to myself.

Galen had given me the keys to his car, but I didn't think he would like to know that she was putting her feet on the dashboard of his car. It was a nice car, and one I could get used to driving it, if he let me. He had two of them, he couldn't drive them both.

"Um...I never really thought too much on it. I like spicy foods." I could see her in the corner of my eye nodding to herself. She had her phone out and was typing on it. I wondered if she was talking to the others, since I wasn't the best at conversing. I was probably boring her.

"Okay, I found a place, then we can maybe wander around. See the sights? I never got a chance the last time I was here...since a dog sniffed me out before I got far." I nodded and smiled.

"Sounds like a great day to me. Just show me the way."

I felt better knowing she was looking up a place to eat, not chatting to the guys. That she was finding something I liked. She was doing something special for me.

I shouldn't have felt jealous, but I knew this was a feeling I would have to deal with over time. I was already starting to feel the shift in the relationship we had. It was just a little harder not to want more alone time with Lexi.

I didn't feel jealous of her giving her kisses to the others. In fact, I'd loved when Ranger was involved yesterday. I didn't know much of what I was doing.

My only knowledge came from watching porn, which wasn't helpful when it came to the real thing. I had asked him for some tips and what to do. I'd felt so stupid when the words had come out of my mouth, but he told me. Then when she agreed to go with us somewhere private, I was so nervous. My hands had been shaking, but with Ranger there we were able to get her off. And that was the best feeling and I couldn't wait to do it again.

We ended up at this little place called Lotus bistro, which served Thai food. I'd never eaten much of this in the past, but I did say I liked spicy food and I could smell the spices as soon as we entered. We chose to eat outside, since it was a nice day, though a little mild, but at least it wasn't raining.

"So I've been thinking, and I didn't know how you would feel about it..." Lexi placed her elbow on the table, and her hand cupped her face as she leaned closer to me. "But I want to get you a gift. Just something small."

I shook my head. "You don't have to do that." She reached across the table and took my hands, and I took a deep breath. She wanted to get me a gift, but... "You are my gift," I told her, and it was true. She was my gift, and might very well be my guardian angel. I liked that theory, and it made sense in some ways, but there were so many other possible reasons why Lexi smelled so good, could heal vampires...could warm them up and hear their thoughts. I hoped that Pack Bardoul would find answers soon, so we knew how to protect her better.

"Let's get green curry. I have always wanted to try it," Lexi said, and I settled back a little in my chair as we ordered. Lexi filled in all the quiet moments, talking about books she'd read, how she felt about graduation and college. All the normal things you would talk about on a date, even though I had never been on one. This was my first, and I loved every moment of it.

My wolf was content, and there was a happy feeling in my chest. After lunch, I took her hand in mine and we went for a stroll along the Olympic Discovery trail. There were other couples out, families, and the day was just so perfect.

"Let's take a photo, now I have a camera phone," Lexi said, and I chuckled as she dragged me towards a bench and pulled me down beside her. I watched as she struggled to find the selfie camera.

"Here, I'll show you." I took it from her and noticed her hands were a little cold as I flipped the camera and pulled her to my side.

"Smile," she said through her teeth as she gave one huge, beautiful grin. I took a few photos before I turned and kissed her cheek and took another. She turned and kissed me, and I took another before dropping my hand and kissing her more deeply.

"You taste like green curry," she said through a laugh, and I didn't know it was possible to smile this much. Then she pulled me back for another kiss.

"No, you taste like green curry...but I like it." I told her as I reached for her again, tasting her, breathing in the fresh sea air and hearing nothing but the deep breathing of my mate as I made out with her.

Suddenly, I could smell a shifter nearby, so I pulled away from Lexi and searched the area. I couldn't see them, but I could smell them. They could just be passing by, but I didn't like it. The smell... I took a deep breath as Lexi held onto me, sensing the change in me. It was a familiar scent, and that had my wolf rising from deep inside me. I let out a low growl that only they could hear.

"Is it a bear shifter?" Lexi whispered as she glanced around. I could smell the fear coming from her, causing an overwhelming need to protect her and working up my wolf. I was shaking, just trying to keep control.

"We need to leave. Now." I could hear a deep chuckle from far away, but he knew I was here. Knew about Lexi. He would've been able to smell her from there.

My uncle had just found me. Just like he said he would.

CHAPTER 25

LEXI

The drive back felt like it took longer than it should have, even though Raff didn't slow down at all. In fact, he was speeding the whole way back. He'd called the others once we were in the car and on our way back to tell them that trouble was in Port Angeles.

So I guessed that meant Raff's birthday dinner with all four of them was now not happening. At least, not away from the Lovell's house. I'd texted Grayson earlier that morning, asking if he could make a cake, and he was more than happy to as he felt guilty missing Raff's birthday also. I was glad I had arranged that at least, I guessed we'd just be blowing out the candles here instead of the restaurant.

When we got to the gate of the Lovell mansion —'cause that's what it was, not a house—it was

Nash and Elijah who were at the gate. I shrunk down a little, because one, Nash, and two, Elijah was Callum's older brother. I still had this horrible feeling that he wasn't happy with me, even though it was me who was bit while doing nothing to provoke it. Just, I didn't know him well, so I wasn't sure what he thought of me. The last thing I wanted was another asshole on my hands.

Raff rolled down the window, and Nash put his big hand on the windowsill as he leaned in, then he looked me and Raff over.

"Galen said to meet at his place." Raff just nodded, then we drove through and parked outside Galen's place. I was glad we were here, since I wasn't in the mood to see Alaric or anyone else.

There were so many men here, older ones that I had never really seen before. I assumed they were the fathers of most these guys. I guessed they were going in for a meeting or something and that was why we were going to Galen's place.

"Lex, holy shit, babe." As soon as I stepped through the door, Ranger had picked me up and spun me around, then he dropped me and looked me over like I was injured. I swatted his arm.

"I'm fine. I didn't know what was going on until we were in the car." Yeah, Raff didn't tell me one of his uncles had spotted us until we were on our way back. I remembered that day in the office, when his uncle had said that Raff belonged to them and that he would kill Shelly, then Raff had said he would come back to them. He'd told them he would return... He probably meant when he turned eighteen, which he was now.

Shit, Shelly. His uncle could have hurt her to find where he was. That had to be the reason he found him—wait, she was a vampire. She wouldn't have done that. They were evenly matched, at least. Plus, she had that shifter cop, Keene, who she was super cozy with... I wondered if she had Stoker, his cop partner too? Huh, I guessed in some ways she was very protected.

At least she'd been right—this was where I belonged. Where we belonged.

Raff was pacing, Maverick was standing awkwardly in the kitchen, and Galen was in the basement. If this wasn't such a stressful situation, I would make a joke or go somewhere less tense. And this was...tense.

"Okay, everyone, sit down. My house is safe to talk in, and we all need to talk."

Galen was up and beside me before I could even blink. My heart skipped a beat, and not in a good way. That was scary as hell when he moved that fast. His hands hovered over me, looking for injuries just like Ranger had.

"I'm fine. But there is some bad shit happening out there, and we need to get this," I gestured to everyone in the room, "worked out before anything else can go forward."

There were some puzzled looks from Ranger and Raff, but Galen knew what I meant. He looked to Maverick, who was now pacing in the kitchen with his hands in his shorts' pockets, looking so wounded. He needed this, even if it was going to be hard to talk about.

"If we're all going to be together, I don't want this weird awkward stuff. We all need to work out our differences. It's important. I'm not asking for you to spill all your secrets. That's not what I am saying. I just need us to be together as one, and that we all trust each other fully.

"Now that Galen is part of this, more so than before, we need to talk. We need to work out what happened between Galen...and Maverick. And then all five of us can grab a bunch of food, veg out, and watch some terrible movies. We'll even let Ranger pick them."

I got a whoop from Ranger, but the others just sat and stared at me, each other, then me again.

"I guess I'll go first? Since I'm the oldest." Galen stood up. Ranger snorted at that, and I rolled my eyes. God, for one minute, could he just behave himself? I pinned him with a glare, and he stopped.

"I want to say that I care for you all. I never thought I would meet someone as special as Lexi. I never thought anything like this could be in the cards. This is new for me, and it may take a little time to get completely used to it. Not only did I get the girl, I got her three shifter mates. Vampires don't have packmates like you do, but I'm glad that the ones I have now are you three." Ranger snorted again, and I grumbled at him under my breath to stop it.

"I'm sorry, it was just a little funny. I've been torturing poor Galen here for *years*, and the fact that we ended up mates to the same gorgeous girl is just a little funny. That was all. But I'm glad he's here. The way you woke up this morning, I could feel it when you knew he was there.

"I guess what I'm saying is, Galen...you complete us." Ranger put his hand on his heart. I thought he was shit stirring and joking around at this important time, but he stood up and walked to Galen, then he wrapped his big arms around him and... hugged him.

"Now that's over, we know Raff totally likes you being here with us too, Galen. But I know the real discussion is not something Raff and I can help with. It's something for the three of you, and I'm happy as long as you all are.

"Mav, I love you. I know you well enough to know that what happened and what was said on

Saturday is affecting you. You all need to talk about it, and now is the best time."

Raff stood up beside Ranger, and the two of them smiled and nodded as they walked out the door, Raff calling out that Ranger wasn't picking the movie.

The silence in the room was deafening. I was just surprised that Ranger said something so... mature. But when no one said anything, it had become a stand-off. I'd thought Maverick was a little more... well, like me. The type to say it like it was. He had no issues telling me to leave Kiba, but he couldn't stand in front of the guy he had a crush on and tell him?

I cleared my throat.

"Let's all take a seat here on the sofa." I took a seat in the middle, in the hope that they might talk more if I was there...like a shield. Because if they couldn't fix this, then this relationship was doomed before we even began.

CHAPTER 26
GALEN

I'd been waiting for this, and I was glad we were doing it now. I had a feeling that Rafferty's uncle wasn't just a once off, that something bigger was going on. When Lexi and Raff were on their way back, I'd had a visitor, but I hadn't told them. I didn't want to worry them at all, but I knew this was somehow linked.

My friend Benedict, he was dying. I hadn't spoken to him for a few weeks, but in that time, he'd met a woman and been attacked by the Russet pack.

Raffety's old pack.

She'd come here to tell me that Ben had tried to call me and that she had tried to call as well. I'd been so distracted that I had missed them and had intended to call him back, but it slipped my mind.

He was dying and had wanted to see me, but at this point, he was past talking. Plus with the threat here, I couldn't leave. As much as I wanted to visit Ben, there was no way I would leave Lexi unprotected. So I gave her a vial of Lexi's blood. It had cured me...more than it should, so a small vial should've been enough. I was still waiting for the call, though it would be nighttime before I found out if it had worked. I truly hoped it did.

Ben, my long-time friend, had found love, only for it to be ripped away too soon. It just showed how quickly your life could be over. I had just found my love, and I didn't want anything stopping us from all being happy. Maverick...he was one of a kind, and I would be lying if I said I wasn't attracted to him. I just...well, I had never been with a shifter before, and I should've spoken to him sooner.

"Okay, let's just start off by saying this is a safe place to express our feelings," Lexi said, facing him. She took his hands and brought them to her lips, then she kissed his knuckles.

When his eyes locked with mine, I could see the swirl of emotion in them. I knew he liked guys as much as girls, but he had kept that secret from so many. It was out in the open on Saturday night when he thought he was losing me.

"I love you," he whispered, and I could see tears in his eyes as he hugged Lexi tight. My heart felt full and overflowing with emotions. This was perfect, this was real, and I knew I would remember this moment for all of time.

"I love you," she whispered back, and I could hear the emotion in her voice.

They kissed, and I watched. It was raw, real...and it made me realize how badly I needed that—what they had now. I watched them as the clock ticked on, until Maverick's eyes found mine. Then it was on. The intensity of his eyes, the way he bit Lexi's lower lip, then licked it and kissed it better, and the whole time, he watched me... It all turned me on, my cock hardened at the sight of them together. I couldn't look away, and when I felt a hand on my knee, skating up my thigh, I sucked in a breath.

"This isn't talking," I mentioned to them, and I could hear Lexi chuckle. Her head lolled back, and she smiled up at me, which made me chuckle.

"Sometimes, actions speak louder than words, Mr. Donovani." I bit my lower lip and growled at her.

"You are a fucking tease...and I love it." I watched her eyes, and the amber in them was glowing as she licked her lips. Maverick didn't let her go as I bent down and took her mouth, my tongue plunging deep, showing her how much I loved her teasing. Her hand curled around my neck as she pulled me closer, taking more from me, and her moans of pleasure went straight to my cock. I shifted, the fabric of my jeans constricting.

"I don't tease, Galen. I know what I want, and I want you...and Maverick. And Ranger and Rafferty.

You're all mine, and we need this to work. If it doesn't, then that's it."

She was smart and wise beyond her years. No seventeen-year-old spoke like this, yet none had been through what she had and now had four mates vying for her attention.

"I want this to work. It will. Maverick and I will work this out. Whatever this is. I promise," I told her, then looked over to him, his eyes swirling. He'd never been so out of control. Did he not want me? Did he regret what he said?

I reached over and pulled his tee, he held fast, his eyes flaring and his breathing heavier.

"Nothing has to happen," I said to Mav. "We're with Lexi, and I'm so blessed to share her with you. If something more was to happen, know that I won't pull away from you. Don't pull away from Lexi. You can come speak to me. Nothing has changed that, Maverick." I could tell he was struggling with emotions he probably didn't yet understand.

This was new to me and to him. Fuck, to all of us. There were some shifters that had brothers as packmates, but there weren't many, and I already felt that Raff and Ranger were happy to do things with Lexi together. Since the pool incident...I'd noticed that Maverick and I had paired off the same way, but I didn't want him to be afraid of me.

"I...I don't know what I want. How far I want to go..." he said, and I nodded as I let go of his tee. He ran his hand down it a few times to straighten it out. His mouth tilted up in a crooked smile as he let out a deep breath. "Fuck, I don't know if I'm gonna regret this." I was puzzled by that, but then he pulled Lexi up and kissed her, hard.

His hand reached out and took my sweater in his fist. I looked down and noticed his knuckles were almost white as he trembled. He pulled and I went, my back flush to Lexi's, then I swept her silky hair to the side and kissed her neck, under her ear... I felt a hand snake up the back of my head, ruffling my hair and holding tight. At first, I thought it was Lexi, but it was too big... My eyes opened wide as Maverick kissed and licked Lexi where I just had. Her hands snaking up my side, I watched as she held him tightly.

She turned and kissed me quickly, licking my lip as she moved back to Maverick. For a while, all I could hear was breathing, moaning, and the racing of hearts, but the scent of them... The lust and love flowing from the both of them was making it hard not to want to go further.

My face was now so close to Mavericks and Lexi's, our breaths mingled in the air between us. She kissed the side of my mouth, then Maverick's, and waited. The tension was thick in the air. I wanted to kiss him, but I was holding off, letting him make the move. If he wanted this, he would have to come to me. Lexi knew what she was doing here—she was pushing Maverick out of his comfort zone. She knew he needed just a little push, but with herself as a safe barrier between us.

I pulled back slightly, wanting to give him space. This was just too fast for him, and we had a forever to work this out. I opened my mouth to tell him it was okay, but before the words came out, his mouth crashed onto mine. I let out a small gasp as he pulled me closer, his tongue finding mine, and I could taste Lexi on his mouth. She was sweet, whereas he was like earth. Fresh, new...

I thought the smell of him would make it hard to kiss him, since I couldn't help being tense around shifters. Even sleeping in the room with them all last night was just as hard for me as it was for Ranger. But it didn't make this hard at all. No, this felt right.

Finally, we pulled apart, our breathing heavy, and Lexi giggled.

"Fuck, that was the hottest thing I've ever seen." My eyes left Maverick's to look at Lexi, and I caught her huge grin. She giggled again.

"Let's go tell the others that you've kissed and made up."

She jumped off the sofa, straightened herself up, and winked at me as she made her way to the door. She turned around and blew a kiss as she opened it, the sunlight streaming in.

"You *coming*, boys?"

The deep chuckle Maverick gave in response was

a sound I'd wanted to hear for days, and I turned to see his dimples out on display, something you didn't see much. Right now, it was perfect, and I knew this wasn't over. But at least I knew that we could move on from here.

"Tease," I muttered as I followed after her, Maverick right on my heels. I watched as she turned to us, her hands in the air as she spun in the sunlight, looking more like an angel than ever.

"You love it...Mr. Donovani." I rolled my eyes, but I couldn't deny it. I loved it...every little bit about her.

CHAPTER 27
LEXI

Okay, if someone had asked me weeks ago if two guys kissing would turn me on, I wouldn't have known. I'd never thought about it. But now that I'd seen it with Maverick and Galen...I couldn't think of anything hotter. With me in the middle, that was even better. I wasn't sure my 'actions not words' thing would work. I didn't know what to really say, and Maverick didn't seem to want to talk. So I did what I thought was best, and it was better than I expected.

"Grayson left this at the gate for you," Jett said, holding a box out to me. Holy shit, Grayson worked fast. I opened it and saw a big, chocolate cake inside. It looked so, so amazing. I looked at the time and could see it was getting very late, it was almost time for dinner.

"We ordered pizza, but we weren't sure how long you would be." I wrapped my arms around Ranger and kissed his cheek. It was a good idea, since I didn't know how long I was going to take with Galen and Maverick so pizza was the best idea.

"Well how long until it arrives? Is there time for cake now?" I was hungry, and I didn't want to wait for cake. I was being a little greedy, but it smelled amazing.

"Don't sing," was all Raff said, his eyes pleading with me. I could see by the tick in his jaw that he really didn't want any more attention, so I gave him a small smile and a nod.

"Cake time." Ranger brought out some plates and a big knife. I handed it to Raff, but he shook his head.

"No, you cut it. I don't want to ruin it."

I didn't need to be told twice and quickly divided it up into six equal pieces. Ranger held out plates as I placed a piece on each of them, and he handed them out to Raff and Maverick. Galen declined, but I was still going to tell him how good it tasted. Jett was still hovering around as Ranger picked up his plate and moaned as he took a bite, his lips covered in chocolate goodness. I reached up, wiped the chocolate from his lips with my thumb, and licked it off. He growled softly at that, and I winked as I turned back to see there were two extra slices.

"Jett," I called out, and he was at my side before I got a chance to finish what I was about to say.

"Yes, dear?" I laughed and rolled my eyes at him. I held up a plate and spun to him, then he reached out and grabbed it.

"Cake?" I asked, I could see his eyes light up playfully as Ranger's growl turned from sexy to downright scary.

"No cake," Ranger said, snatching the plate away, and it landed with a loud clang on the dark granite countertop. Oh my god, not again. "You cannot have cake. Lexi has no more slices left to give, and she has all the cake she needs."

Galen was between them fast, and I could tell Ranger was getting close to shifting. Jett just shook his head, his hands in the air as he backed away from us. Lyell had entered the kitchen just at that moment and looked at the scene in front of him. I wasn't too sure if he would step in and help, or run back to his room. He was...different from his brothers, and I didn't know what he was thinking ever. He probably regretted coming in the kitchen right now.

"Fucking hell, Ranger. It's just cake," I yelled. It was...wasn't it? What did I do? I just didn't get it. There was plenty of cake to go around, and Jett was here, so I offered some to him. Honestly, I didn't think it would set Ranger off like this.

I thought we'd had this talk about jealousy and that Ranger understood that I wasn't doing anything with Jett. Fuck, he was still in love with Clare. That much was obvious when I was with Jett last week, since he spoke about her non-stop.

"Ranger. You know I wouldn't take *your* slice. I love Lexi, as a sister. That's it. Seriously, brother. It was just cake, nothing more. I promise you that. You're working shit up in your mind that's not there. Fuck, do you have zero faith in me? In Lexi?"

I could see Ranger's eyes flicking between us all. Maverick went to him and held his shoulder, then Rafferty did the same. I just stood there, confused, upset, while he looked at me, his eyes now glassy. He was breathing heavy, his shoulders slumped, and I watched the tension leave him.

"I trust you, I do. My wolf just gets territorial, but I was okay with it all. Okay?" He shrugged the guys off and took a step to me. "It was the cake... Lexi wanted to have her cake and eat it too...and I just...I took it the wrong way when you gave a slice to Jett. I'm sorry. I'm trying so hard here, and I keep fucking it up, but my wolf... it's so hard."

Ranger was a bag of strong emotions that he couldn't hide from, and he really had a different way of showing it. It was just cake. I liked Jett, he was fun, but I was in love with Ranger. What I had with him was never going to change, just like my feelings for Jett were never going to change.

"I love you. I've taken all the slices of cake I need,

okay? I have a whole cake now." His forehead gently nudged mine as he took a deep breath.

"I love you to the moon and back, Lex. I keep fucking this up, and I want to say this will be the last time, I do. But even I know that would be a lie. My wolf is hard to control, and I react without thinking. But I will try. For you."

I stood up on my toes and kissed him, wrapping my arms around his neck and pulling him down. I could taste the chocolate on his lips and tongue as his hands skated down my back to cup my ass. He pulled me closer to him, and it felt like he was trying to tell me through actions how much I meant to him and how sorry he was for snapping at his brother. He tugged me up, and I smiled as I jumped, wrapping my legs around him.

I pulled away slightly and looked down at him now. It was nice to be high up, since I seemed to always be the shortest around here.

"No more, okay? Mr. big bad Wolfy needs to behave, or I won't stroke him anymore." There were groans and some chuckles around us.

Jett came up and put his hand on Ranger's shoulder. He tensed slightly under me, but he seemed to be more relaxed now.

"So, we good?" Jett asked, and Ranger nodded, squeezing my ass. I let out a squeak and felt his deep chuckle through his chest. Then he turned to Jett.

"Have some cake, it's really good.... Happy birthday, Rafferty."

And everyone called out happy birthday to Raff, he was all shy and bashful looking at the attention. I loved it.

And it was really good cake. Grayson was a genius.

CHAPTER 28
LEXI

Galen walked me to my room, and it brought back memories of him and I after my first night at the Lovell's house and the terrible dinner guest I was. Well...they did ask for it by basically kidnapping me. Except this time, there was nothing stopping him from kissing me...or from coming in and staying with me.

I smiled as I held onto the brass handle. I could feel him, inches from me, his breath heating my neck.

I wasn't sure what was going on or why we weren't all coming in here. We'd spent the evening watching movies, ones that I made sure Raff had a choice in picking. He really liked superheroes, but they all did. At least the actors they choose for these roles were hot, which was the only thing that kept my eyes open.

I opened the door, expecting him to follow, but then the click of the door and the cold in the room told me I was alone. The white walls seemed to get closer the longer I was in here with my thoughts. I shook off the feeling and used this chance to have a shower and get comfy.

When I got out of the shower, towel wrapped around me, I bounced out into my room, hoping to find a bed full of guys. But it was empty. I was so confused now, and my heart sank a little. Did I do something wrong? I thought we were all having a great night celebrating Raff's birthday.

In my closet, I picked out a tank to wear. I hesitated at first, but then decided to wear my new lace thong. I had plans to show a little cheek. I pulled up a pair of sleep shorts to keep it tame, in case I saw someone else, and returned my towel to the bathroom. I didn't know what to do with myself, so I flopped onto the bed and rolled over to the side table. I picked up my Kindle and started looking for a book to read, but I couldn't concentrate.

I had told Raff he was sleeping with me tonight and always. I wasn't ever going to sleep alone again. But instead...I was here in my room, alone, and it was just...quiet. Too quiet.

Shit, I'd forgotten about his uncle. Were Raff's uncles here, trying to take him away? Was that why I was in here alone? Before I could work myself up any more, there was two knocks at the door. I jumped and spun on the bed, watching as it opened.

My hand went to my chest, and I let out a deep breath.

"Oh, Maverick. You scared me."

He looked around the room, his face worrying me more.

"Shit, Lexi, are you okay?"

I looked around the room too. Did someone break in? I didn't like the space between us, so I crossed the room faster than I ever had. I held onto him, and he wrapped his arms around me.

"What happened?" I asked him. He looked down at me as he pushed some hair that had fallen across my face behind my ear.

"Nothing. We were just giving Raff some Kiba birthday love is all. Turning eighteen is a huge deal here. So we just...you know...welcomed him to the pack." He smiled, his dimples flashing for a brief moment. Dimples...they were my thing! He chuckled and hugged me tighter to his chest, and I breathed in his fresh pine scent.

"As much as I want to stay here, just you and me, I'm here to take you over to Galen's." I tilted my head up at him.

"Why? Is everything okay?" I was worried, but when he skated his foot along the carpet, I swear he was blushing.

"Just, you know. More private there." I felt

relieved. That was why, and I guessed it made sense. Alaric wasn't happy with me spending the night with them. That was why he had Jett follow me around so much last week. So at least at Galen's, it was his house. His rules. Right? And he had the thing where people couldn't hear us, so we could... Oh.

"Oh, yes. I'll just grab a few things."

IT WAS A FAST TRIP OVER, and Maverick gave me a piggyback ride so I didn't have to put on shoes. He didn't even need to open the door, since the guys were already there and waiting. Maverick let go of my legs and I lowered myself to the floor, but not before dragging my body down his muscular back and feeling it in the best way. I clenched my thighs together. They were all there and watching me, taking me in. I wanted a special birthday someone to touch me...*now*.

"Hey, Lex, you smell good." Ranger purred. I knew what he was talking about, and I shoved him playfully. He grabbed my arm, spun me to him, and growled "Mine" into the nape of my neck, he rubbed against my neck... marking me after my shower. I kissed him quickly before I ran over and jumped into Raff's lap. I think I surprised him at the move. He grabbed my ass and squeezed, and I couldn't help but rub myself against him. I needed the friction and I needed Rafferty King.

"Alright, that's our cue to leave." Galen twirled his finger around, and I watched the three of them get up to leave. *"You look so fucking sexy... I can tell you're wearing that lace thong, and it is taking every ounce of willpower to walk out this door right now."* I glanced back at Galen, and heat flooded my body, going straight to my core. I was wet, but now... Fuck. Cheeky asshole nodded at us, a crooked smile on his face.

Ranger winked and blew me a kiss, but it was Raff who surprised me when he reached up and caught it. I could hear the laughter as Ranger closed the door behind them.

I grabbed his closed fist and opened his hand. "I think you took something from me." I watched as a grin slowly formed on his lips.

"Ranger blew me a birthday kiss. This one is mine." This was perfect. After the horrible moment after lunch, I'd worried he would regress a little, but he was being playful and cute. I liked this Raff, he had really come out of his shell here.

I wrapped my arms around his neck, leaned down, and kissed him. I swept my tongue inside his mouth, and he tasted like peppermint. I pulled back and eyed him for a moment. He just lay his head back on the couch and palmed my ass through my sleep shorts.

"What?" he asked, but I could sense a hint of nerves in his voice. His hands ran up the back of my tank and flared on my lower back. They were warm on my cooler skin. I had an idea of what was happening here. Why they'd left and we were here, with soundproof walls surrounding us.

"Did you want to take this to the bedroom?" I asked, and his blue eyes swirled. He closed them briefly, and when his eyes opened, he glanced to the bedroom door. It was open, and I was sure we were allowed to use it.

CHAPTER 29
RAFFERTY

Fuck, I was so nervous. I didn't want to fuck this up, and the guys had spent almost an hour telling me things, like what to do, what not to do. I was so confused, until Galen stepped up and told me that every woman was different and not to listen just to Ranger. He said to ask Lexi what she likes, and if she liked something, I would know. She would make sure I did.

Then again, this was only wishful thinking, since I wasn't expecting to have sex tonight. Only if she wanted to. I'd wanted to make love to Lexi since the day I first saw her and those huge amber eyes looked onto mine. I was reckless, and I'd marked her and got beat up over and over. But it was worth it, for this moment alone.

I'd known since that day, when my hands were cuffed behind my back, sitting there waiting for

Shelly to take us to this foster house she had always talked about. That was when I had this over-whelming need to protect Lexi, it washed through me to hard. She needed someone, even though she didn't know it. I didn't know it at the time either, but my wolf knew it. He knew she was mine, and that I would die for her.

Even now, my wolf wanted her to accept him, to bond with him. I knew that couldn't happen, and I knew he sensed that too. It was instinct, something driven in me that would never go away. Over time, my wolf would understand that you don't need a bond to be in love.

I had her on the soft bed. Galen had changed the sheets and lit a candle to try and help with his smell. It wasn't so bad, but the scent of Lexi's lust was stronger. Her hand snaked down between us as she took the hem of my T-shirt and pulled it up. I stood back and took it off, baring my chest to her, hoping she would see the fresh ink I had done last week. It was hard with the guys always wanting to shift, but I held it off just in time. I had to get it done fast, before I turned eighteen.

I took her hand and ran it down over my chest and stopped. Her smile was lazy as I took her finger and ran it over the words.

"Lexi my heart," I whispered to her, and she reached her other hand up and pulled herself up. She looked down to my chest, and I could tell the moment she saw it. She gasped, her finger running over the words so lightly, it tickled.

"Holy shit, when...?" I could hear her voice crack. Shit, I didn't want to make her cry. Her face was a little flushed, but I could see the tears forming in her eyes.

"Shhh...don't cry, Lexi. You have my heart, and it beats every day. For you." She choked out a small sob and wiped some tears away. Fuck, was I fucking this up? I had no idea what to do.

"Rafferty, I love you. You have my heart, always... forever." Her voice cracked again, but before I spoke a word, she took my mouth, her hunger for me just as deep as mine. My cock strained in my shorts, as I laid her back down on the bed and pushed her up into the middle. She giggled as I crawled on the bed and stalked her, her legs opening for me to fit between them.

"Too many clothes, what do you think?" she asked, and I nodded as I watched Lexi pull her tank off. She wasn't wearing anything under it, and her sweet, pink nipples were tight as she arched towards me.

I cupped one breast, kneading it as I took her nipple between my lips and sucked gently, her breasts were such a perfect size for me. Her fingers splayed in my hair as I licked and sucked. I took the other nipple, my hips moving on their own and grinding my erection against the heat of her core.

God, I needed to slow down, or I would come too soon.

I pulled back and looked down at her beneath me, her chest falling and rising fast. She took my hand and placed it between her breasts, then slowly pushed it down, further and further, until it was at her waistband. She slid her finger underneath and pushed. My hand gripping the fabric, I pulled them down. I moved back as I did, exposing her wet core to me.

When I scrambled back up, she placed a hand on my chest to stop me. My heart was beating out of my chest, and I could smell her arousal, her lust. I wanted to taste her. I wanted my mouth on her clit. I wanted her to call out my name as I pushed her over the edge into a earth shattering orgasm.

"Raff, let me take off your shorts." I moved so she could undo my button and fly. She tried to pull them down, but my erection was straining in my boxers and making it hard to move them. So I jumped back, took a deep breath, and pulled it up and over, pushing them to the floor. I hesitated at first before I looked back to Lexi.

Her elbows were propping her up, her pink swollen lip between her teeth as she sucked in a breathy moan.

My wolf wanted to strut. He was pleased that she liked what she saw. She crooked her finger and gestured for me to come to her, and I jumped up.

The bed made a sound of protest at the movement, and it made Lexi giggle.

"Kiss me," she said and I leaned down and kissed her lips. I moved down her neck, her chest, making sure to lick and suck on each nipple, and it made her cry out, her body arching into my hands. I dipped my tongue in her belly button and swirled before I got to the source of the most amazing smell I'd ever known. I placed a small kiss at the top, and her hand went straight to my hair as her hips bucked up, legs spreading wider. "God, Raff. Lick my clit."

I ran my finger between her folds, making sure to touch her sensitive clit on the way down, and dipped inside her warm, wet pussy. As she moaned my name again, I licked and sucked her clit, teasing and tormenting her until her hand tightened on my hair. Her legs started to shake, and she called out, clamping her knees to my head. I kissed and sucked and fucked her with my fingers as she rode out her orgasm.

My cock was so hard, pre-cum was leaking onto the sheets as I ground my cock into the mattress. I didn't want to touch myself. I would come before it was all over, and I didn't want that to happen.

"I want to suck your cock so bad, Rafferty." The way she said my name sounded like silk on her tongue. I wanted that too, but I wanted to be inside her more.

I pulled back off the bed and opened the draw that Galen had shown me earlier. I pulled out a foil square and moved back over to Lexi. I handed it to her, since I was giving her the choice of what we did. If this was all we did, I'd be just as happy as if we went all the way. She smiled and took the foil between her teeth and ripped it open.

"I want to make love to you," I whispered, but I knew that no one else could hear us. My heart was pounding in my chest, and with the taste of her on my tongue, my cock was going to explode from excitement before she even came near it.

"I want to make love to you too." She took the rubber in her hand and, pinching the tip, she moved her hands. She palmed the underside of my cock, and I hissed out, gritting my teeth and trying to stop myself from coming. She placed the condom on over the head, and with one hand, rolled it down to the base. It felt tight, and I was trying so hard to think of anything but her hand on my cock. When she cupped my balls, I quickly moved away. She tilted her head, and the wicked grin on her lips had me eyeing her. She giggled, and I shook my head.

"A little close, are we?"

I nodded. "You are so sexy, Lexi, and you taste better than I ever imagined. I just want to make this last. I don't want to... blow too early." That had been my biggest fear, but Lexi just shrugged.

"We can always do it again if you do. I'm so

worked up that this might be fast for me too." She stroked my hair with the tips of her fingers, and I took three deep breathes before I moved towards her again. She laid down on her back, her legs open, and I settled between them. I moved my hips, rubbing against her as we kissed.

She reached between us, and I pulled back to watch as she took my cock, my pulse picking up as I felt her place me at her entrance. I looked down between us as I moved my hips slowly, as I entered her it was warm and tight, making me groan loudly.

"Fuck, holy shit," I hissed out as I slowly filled her to the hilt.

"I love you, Lexi." I kissed her, soft and sweet, then I pulled my hips back and slowly moved in again. The feeling was nothing I could describe. This felt more than just pleasure... it was coming home, where I belonged.

"I love you, Rafferty." Her hand on my ass pulled me as deep as I could go.

I watched again as I slowly made love to her, her thumb brushing over her clit as I started to pick up speed.

"Fuck, oh fuck, I'm close." Her moaning got louder as I placed more of my weight on her, pulling her close to me as I ground against her clit, the rhythm getting faster. I felt the tightness in my balls as the orgasm raced down my spine. My body trembled as I rode out the intensity of my climax.

I sagged against her, my arms lifting myself off her enough to make sure I wasn't crushing her. Our breaths were both heavy, her nipples brushing against my chest at the movements. I kissed her over and over, so grateful I waited for this moment with her. She was my first hug, first kiss, and now, she'd taken my virginity.

I rolled over onto my side, taking the condom off and tying off the end like Ranger told me. I threw it in the direction of the trash can. I turned back and pushed her hair behind her ear. She smiled lazily, her eyes struggling to stay open.

"That was amazing, thank you for letting me be your first," she said, her hand running down my chest and tracking my tatts. I couldn't get enough of her fingers touching my bare skin.

I closed my eyes at the feeling as I relaxed into the mattress and wrapped my body around hers, hugging her tightly to me. The air in the room was a little chilly on my body, so I thought she might be cold too. I pulled up what I could of the bed covers and threw it over us.

"I love you," I whispered. Then I fell asleep with the love of my life in my arms.

CHAPTER 30
LEXI

I woke up, my muscles feeling good, and stretched my arms above my head, letting out a deep sigh as I snuggled down deep into the comforter. Last night was so amazing, there were no words. I reached out, hoping to find Raff so maybe I could get a little morning sex in, but no one was there. I opened my eyes and looked around the room.

Galen's room was so beautiful. The dark wood really made a statement, it stood out, but I guessed if you live in a house as white as the Lovell's, everything that had color looked beautiful.

"Raff?" I called out. The bedroom door was ajar, and I could hear someone out there. Did the guys stay out all last night? I pulled the comforter back and saw I was wearing a white T-shirt, so I brought it to my nose and inhaled. *Maverick*. Huh.

I made my way out of bed and to the bedroom door, hesitating a bit, as I didn't have any underwear on. But the T-shirt was long enough to cover me if someone like Alaric or Nash were out in the living room. Which I really hoped they weren't. I poked my head around and looked into the kitchen. I could see a bottle of whiskey and an empty glass beside it.

"Galen?" I called out, holding the hem of the shirt as I padded barefoot out and into the kitchen. My stomach rumbled, I was really hungry. When wasn't I hungry, should really be the question. I opened his fridge to see what he had in there and found a huge platter of tiny triangle sandwiches, all different types. I was sure he wouldn't mind if I snuck one or two. I grabbed two, one with cheese and the other had some chicken and mayo.

I grabbed a glass and filled it with tap water, then took a seat on his stool. The coldness sent a little shiver though me, and I laughed a little as half of my bare ass was sitting on it. That was kind of wrong, but it felt a little naughty too. When the front door opened and Galen's face appeared, I felt... relief.

I guessed I was a little upset at not waking up next to Raff, or anyone for that matter. I was finding I didn't like being alone anymore, at all, and this morning just proved that.

"Good afternoon, sleepy head. Glad to see you're

up...and eating the lunch I made for you and the others." I pushed the rest of the sandwich into my mouth and smiled around it. Galen chuckled and made his way to me. His hand went behind my neck, pulling it forward, and he planted a soft kiss on my forehead.

With my mouth half full, I asked where the others were. Galen took the sandwiches out of the fridge and placed them in front of me.

"Well, they waited for as long as they could, but you were exhausted, so I told them I would be here. I'm sorry I wasn't here when you woke up."

They couldn't wait for me? I felt a little hurt. What where they doing this early?

"Where did they go?" Galen took a sandwich piece and placed it just in front of my mouth. I smiled as I took a bite. It was so yummy. So good.

"They have to take turns in protection. It's ramped up more now we know that Russet has taken an interest in Rafferty...and you." I coughed, almost choking on the food. I took a mouthful of water, since my throat felt tight. I was worried. Raff had been so scared yesterday when he saw his uncle. We didn't talk about it last night, but I knew it was still on his mind.

"So they got the early shift?" That sucked. Galen shook his head and pointed behind him at a clock on the wall. It said it was just after one o'clock. That couldn't be right, that thing had to be broken. I didn't sleep that long.

"You slept in. An *angel* like you needs her beauty sleep." My mouth dropped open as I turned back to Galen.

"Wh...what? Are you for real?" He smiled and rounded back to me, his hands landing on my waist as my legs parted for him to step closer, revealing myself to him. His eyes never left mine though as he held me tight.

"Pack Bardoul came this morning. They have strong reason to believe that yes, you are part angel. Your blood is not human, and it's not shifter or vampire. They've been in contact with a warlock, who has given them indication that the angel idea is the correct one. They're trying to work with him, since he knows of an angel, and they're doing everything they can to meet with her and hopefully compare blood if she lets them. We don't believe you are from a full angel, that you might be a quarter or even less."

I just stared at Galen for a good minute. I was an angel. *Holy shit.* Oh shit, I shouldn't say holy, should I? Oh god, I was fucking this up bad. *Oh, shit.*

"There aren't many angels... Well, we don't think there are. Otherwise, we would all know about them, right? We hope to locate your father. Maybe he can help you with your powers and what to expect. I think our sharing of blood and the shifter venom triggered something in you, but we haven't seen what you can really do. So..."

He pushed back my hair as my heart raced. They were going to try to find my father. My real one. What if he didn't want me? He had left me behind already, why would he want to meet me now? My stomach was in knots, and I felt sick. I didn't know what to say. Galen had made it sound so...good. His hands ran up and down my arms before he embraced me in a tight hug, and I noticed he was warm.

"My beautiful Lexi. I didn't think how finding your biological father would affect you. Please forgive me. I should have asked you if you wanted us to find him." I cleared my throat, but my tongue felt thick and words wouldn't come. It didn't take long before Galen took me from the stool. He pulled the T-shirt down and covered my ass before carrying me to the sofa.

"Shh... It's normal to feel this way. Okay?" I nodded, not knowing what to say.

I was an angel, and I had a father out there, somewhere, who abandoned me and left me with a childhood of fucked-up trauma, never once coming to my rescue. On the nights when the foster home would get bad, I would dream that one day, someone would come rescue me. But in the end, you didn't need a knight, you just needed yourself. I didn't need this angel to tell me who I was, or what I was. I already knew.

I was Lexi Turner. I had almost completed high school. I would graduate and go to college, make something of myself, and have supportive, caring men by my side till the day I died. Yeah, I had made those kinds of plans. I'd always laughed at girls who did, but I knew I didn't want to be anywhere else.

Galen's arms were like magic, helping me to remember who I was. I was strong, and I could work this angel stuff out for myself.

"I don't need him," I said. "I can do this without him. Can we like, practice my angel-ness? Can I warm up your arm again?"

Galen's eyes widened, and he didn't look like he was jumping at the chance to try out my heating abilities anytime soon.

"Or...we could try something else?" I said with a shrug. I watched as he ran his tongue along his bottom lip. Oh...we could try anything. Kissing would be a good one. I moved towards him, but his finger pressed against my mouth. I pouted and he chuckled. I loved to hear him laugh.

"Get dressed. You have some clothes on the dresser. We'll go bring the guys some lunch, and you can practice your angel-ness outside, in private. Preferably on Ranger first." I laughed, and he just winked at me. "But you can't mention it out there, okay? We don't want any prying ears overhearing it."

I nodded and he dropped his finger, so I made my move and kissed him quickly. I jumped up and made my way into his bedroom, then turned to see him watching me. Just before I stepped inside, I flicked the hem of the T-shirt up and flashed him my bare ass. He made a groaning sound, and I smiled to myself, my body reacting to his sounds as I closed the door and stroked my tight nipples through the soft fabric. I felt it instantly between my legs and clamped them together.

"Hurry up, or I will come in and spank you."

I froze, heat flaring all over my body at his words. He must have drunk my blood again. I smiled, since I liked that so much. I love hearing him like this, he always seemed to give me the dirty thoughts, ones he wouldn't speak out loud.

"I'm not joking, Lexi. I don't hear you dressing, and we're already late," he called out from the other room. Just that alone made me want to be a little naughty and see if he really would spank me. I giggled when he called out again and decided it would be more fun to meet up with the guys smelling like this.

CHAPTER 31
RANGER

I was sitting beside Saint, who was swapping over with me so I could meet up with Galen and Lex for lunch, but they'd been taking too long. I hadn't wanted to leave her in bed this morning. When we got back into that room last night, fuck, it was hard not to rub one out. Maverick took his T-shirt off and gave it to Raff, who dressed Lex in it so she wasn't naked. I didn't have a problem with her nudity, but when I'd dropped everything to jump in with them all, I got pushed out and onto the cold floor.

Turned out, none of them were into sleeping naked. Well at least not me naked.

"So, what's going on with you and Ada?" Saint was Mav's best friend, but that didn't mean we weren't close friends like they were. We told each other shit, but we never spoke about Mav, which was what made this friendship work. I could ask him about girls, though. Especially about what the hell was going on with him, Noah, and Ada, because that was looking like a TV drama in the making. And one I kinda liked to watch.

"Nothing. I'm just making sure Noah keeps some boundaries is all. She's hung up on his age, thinks he's too young for her, and I just don't want to see him get hurt." My eyes shifted to read his face, because that smelt like a lie. Even my wolf knew that he was lying, but I didn't want to push him on the matter. I was just curious, was all.

"It's only two years, but he is immature. He would need to grow up fast. Plus, Ada is..." I didn't have words to say what I thought of Ada. Yeah, she was a great friend to Lex and I liked her for that, but if she wasn't her friend, I would've avoided her. She was just so... "Bossy?" Shit, was that even the right word? "A perfectionist? Demanding?"

Pain shot through my chest, and I wheezed for breath.

"The fuck, man?" I asked after I'd caught my breath, rubbing the pain with my hand. Saint had hit me. *Hard*.

"Stop speaking shit about her," Saint growled.

My brows raised at that. Oh yeah, he was lying when he'd said nothing was going on. He liked her. I smirked at him.

"Meet us at the cliffs." I heard Galen say to me...

us. Mav and Raff were working the other side, but Noah and one of his fathers were going to take over for them. I hated having to leave Lex to protect her out here. I wanted to stay with her and keep her safe, but it was agreed that Galen would do that while we three had to take protection shifts.

I stood up and clapped Saint on his shoulder.

"Nothing, my ass," I whispered, just before I shifted. I grabbed my shorts in my mouth, hoping I didn't put any holes in them, and ran towards the cliffs, to the edge of Kiba territory where it meets the Sea. It was a huge drop, and not one I liked to be near. Heights weren't really my thing.

As I entered the clearing, Lexi was sitting on a blanket with her back to me, her hair was loose, and the golden-brown strands blowing in the sea wind. She laughed at something Mav said to her. I dropped my shorts and let out a sound to let her know I was here, in wolf form, since I didn't want to scare her again. I would never forgive myself for that. My wolf was starting to realize that I needed to think before acting on instinct.

I was rewarded by a huge smile.

"Ranger, oh my gosh," she squealed as she turned to me, and I couldn't hold my wolf back any longer. He wanted to be stroked by his mate. With her hand out, I brought my head down and butted against it, her fingers scratching deep into my fur. She lifted her hand to move away, but I wasn't having it. I moved in closer, placing my neck on her shoulder and pawing at her for more.

"Seriously?" Mav growled, but I didn't care. She wrapped her arms around me, hugging me tight, and I was happy. This was so good, and my wolf needed it, especially after she'd said she wouldn't pet him anymore if I didn't behave. These moments were too good not to behave. A tug at my ear had me moving back from Lexi, and I chose that moment to shift back.

"Wow." The word whooshed out of Lexi's mouth, and I couldn't help the huge grin I was sporting at that. I stood up, my huge frame blocking out the sun as she checked me out.

Hands on my hips, I let her have a good eye full at how she made me feel. My wolf really liked being stroked by his mate, and the evidence was clear.

She held up her finger and thumb with an inch between them and said, "Bit chilly?" and the guys burst into laughter. I pointed at Lex, arching my brow and she burst into giggles.

"Well, I'm glad I made you all laugh." And I was. I didn't want to see Lex worried or upset today. Galen would have told her the news, and a little teasing about my dick was worth it for the smile on her face. I picked up my shorts and pulled them on before settling beside her.

"I made sure they didn't eat them all," she said, handing me some sandwiches on a small plate, and my heart swelled in my chest. I should've known by now that she cared about me a lot. I knew this, even though my wolf had fears that she would leave, but just her thinking about me like this got me right in the heart. I was so in love with this girl.

"OKAY, let's have some fun. Ranger, you want to be the first I practice on?" I was standing now, back from the edge of the cliff. The birds were calling out over the water, and it was a nice day, even though the breeze had a chill.

"Hell yeah." I was surprised she'd picked me to try out her powers on first, but I walked over to her and she took my hands. I looked into her beautiful amber eyes, the gold flecks in them sparkling, and watched as her gorgeous face twisted in concentration. I waited for something to happen, but there was nothing. She turned back to Galen, who watched her with such intensity, then she nodded.

They were doing that mind talk thing, so maybe that would be a good one to try? Like maybe she could hear my thoughts.

Lex, Lex, Lex... I watched her face, but there was no change. She let out a huff and dropped my hand.

"Nothing is working." She seemed deflated, but we'd only been trying for a minute. I didn't want her to give up that easy. I was still so happy to be picked first, I didn't want to be the one not working.

"Hey, what were you trying to do? Maybe try something else?" I grabbed her hand before she could turn away.

"I was trying to do the warm thing on you." I nodded. Okay, but I was already warm. Galen was cold. That was what she said, that he was cold and she felt bad that he was and then she heated his arm.

"Well, I am warm. Maybe try making me cold?" I suggested. The others started talking, agreeing.

"Or make him shift? Push his wolf out...not that it's hard too." Maverick suggested.

I held my hands up in the air and backed up a step. "Hang on. I don't want anyone fucking with my wolf." And that was the truth. I wasn't sure what her powers were, but I didn't want to mess with that.

"I won't mess with your wolves. I love them, and I hope to be in a huge puppy pile later on."

Now that was something I wanted too. I could lay beside her every day in wolf form. I pulled her in for a bear hug, and she melted in my arms.

"Okay, practice on me. I would do anything to help you, Lex."

I bent down and kissed the tip of her nose, which was a little cold. I watched her lips as she pursed them together, then a hint of a smile twisted her mouth. Oh man, she was planning something, and I wasn't sure I would like it.

What had I agreed to?

CHAPTER 32
LEXI

Okay, I was thinking some pretty funny thoughts about what I could do to Ranger, but this was hard. I'd just thought I could heat his arm up and then move on to a new thing, but it was proving harder than I thought. Not that I had tried it since that day, but maybe I should try the cold thing.

"Concentrate. Will it because you want it."

Having Galen in my head was also a little distracting, but he was right. I was trying so hard to will it. I tried to think about cold, willing his hands to go cold, but they were big and warm in mine. I let out a growl of frustration.

"You got this, Lex." I rolled my eyes at his nickname for me, but I'd given up on correcting him. Huh, maybe instead of making him cold...I could give him ants in his pants? Like he had something tickling him all over...

I smiled and watched his face. He looked worried, but I was going to have too much fun if I could do this. I closed my eyes and thought of little ants walking all over him, tickling his skin. Even the thought was making my skin crawl. Then his hands pulled away from me fast.

"Nope, fuck this. Nope. Nope. It's tingling all over... What the hell, Lex?"

I opened my eyes and saw he was twisting and shaking his body. I turned to Galen, and saw he was watching in fascination. Raff's mouth was dropped open, and Maverick's eyes crinkled as his grin grew huge.

"What did you do to him?" Maverick asked, and the humor in his voice had me choke out a small laugh.

"Lexi, you did something. What did you think about?" Galen asked in that teacher type voice of his. I watched Ranger running his arms over his legs. Shit. I didn't think about how long it would last for.

"I thought of little ants crawling over his body and tickling him." Ranger's eyes widened as his mouth dropped.

"I... Fuck, it worked, but I'm not going again. Nope, it's all over. They feel like they're in my ass crack." He shook his whole body, then dropped his shorts and shifted in front of me. Galen came and held my shoulders as we watched Ranger shake his fur out, then in less than ten seconds, he was back to Ranger again.

"Okay, so that wasn't so bad, now that I've shifted. I feel like I did my part of the day as the guinea pig...so Mav is up next. Bring his wolf out." Ranger shoved Maverick towards me, but he didn't seem to care. He took my hands in his and looked down at me.

"Give it your best shot," he said, then he winked.

WE SPENT the afternoon trying out different things. Ants crawling worked on all of them. Galen was still smiling and nodding as if nothing was happening, but he seemed to wear the effects the longest. The other guys just had to shift, and the power wore off. Galen was curious to see if I could compel, but that didn't work.

I would be lying if I said I didn't try and *will* wings... I wanted to fly. So when they were talking about something new to try, I would concentrate on wings, growing wings and flying high. By the time dinner rolled around, my stomach rumbled and I was so tired, I just wanted to stuff my face and crawl into bed.

Galen had let me ride on his back to this spot. It was beautiful, and I knew I wanted to come back. It was a direct line to the Lovell place, so it would be easy to find again. I jumped on his back, and he ran at vampire speed back to the house, where a nice meal had been set up and all the Lovells were sitting around the table, waiting for us. We all piled in, my eyes barely staying open, and Galen moved his chair closer so I could rest my head on his shoulder. It was either him or Raff, since the twins were too tall for me to do that.

Alaric stood at the head of the table, and everyone looked to him. It was hard to read his expression, since he always looked so serious.

"Welcome officially to the family, Rafferty King. You are now Pack Kiba. We will protect you, as you protect us."

Everyone clapped, and I joined in. Jett wrapped his arm around Raff's shoulder and pulled him in for a side hug. There were lots of congratulations and 'one of us' comments.

I smiled as I watched them all together. This was what being in Pack Kiba was—a family. I took a bite of roasted potato and quietly chewed, then placed my fork on my plate and lay my head against Galen's shoulder again. I took a deep breath and rested my eyes.

Just for a moment.

CHAPTER 33
LEXI

It was so warm and soft and hard... *Hard?* There was something very hard poking me in the back. I grinned and arched back, my arm going up behind me and snaking around Raff's neck.

A hand slid around my middle and pulled me closer, his body rubbing against my ass a few times, and I chuckled. I tipped my head back and took a deep breath, but what I assumed was Raff didn't smell like him, so I cracked opened an eye and saw two green ones looking down at me.

I gave a lazy smile at Ranger...and I remembered this position very well from when we were in the pool. Only we were missing someone. I glanced around, seeing we were in my bedroom, but Raff wasn't here.

"Morning wood?" I asked, and he gave me that cocky smile, then ground his erection into my ass.

"It is a good morning. I never get to be the one waking up alone next to you. I can see why Raff loves it so much," he replied. It was a surprise to find him in my bed without the others, but now they had all these protection shifts it would be a while before we all were waking up together. But I wasn't complaining. This was a nice, more than nice. I moved against him, teasing and giving more pressure, and he moaned.

"Do you tease me to torment me? Like how I thought I was special yesterday when you picked me first to try your skills out on?" I started to laugh. Shit, I bet Galen told him.

Before I could say anything, he took my chin between his thumb and knuckle, tilting it up, and took my mouth. Our tongues went from lazy to waging a war... He was upset with me, I could feel that, but I turned him on too much to care as our tongues danced and clashed, my body hyper aware of his. This was the best way to wake up.

His hands traveled my body, the exposed skin sending me wild. God, he was amazing at this. This boy knew how to kiss and all the right buttons to push. His fingers trailed up my thigh, higher and higher, until they reached my sleep shorts and made their way under.

He hesitated, waiting for permission, but I wanted this. I needed this.

"Ranger...touch me." I gasped as his hand slid

over my underwear and I ground myself into his palm. I wanted more friction, I needed... "More." I felt his chuckle before he removed his hand and started to push the T-shirt I was wearing up higher. He moved down and kissed my belly, then rubbed his neck and head against my bare skin, and I laughed.

"Are you marking me?" I asked.

His smile was a little devilish, his hair all messed up, but those green eyes were gorgeous. There was no denying that.

"While you're down there..." His brow raised, but he didn't need convincing. His tongue dipped out and onto my heated skin, then he slowly licked his way down to the waistband of my shorts, sending the most amazing sensation to my clit. God...please. I pressed my hand on his head, letting him know I wanted more.

"Oh, is this what you want?" he asked as he started to pull my shorts down, and I did everything to help remove them faster. He chuckled. "Someone needs a lesson in patience"

I shook my head. I didn't need to learn anything, I just needed something, and he was going to give it to me. With four hot as fuck boyfriends, my libido was at an all-time high, and last night with Raff only woke it up more.

When Ranger pressed a kiss on the outside of my underwear, his hot breath set me off and I bucked beneath him. God, how did that feel so... "Fuck," I moaned.

"More? You need more?"

Just like a wolf, I growled at him, "Stop teasing me, or I'll find someone who will do it." His thumbs hooked my underwear and dragged them down, and I lifted my hips so they could come off. I watched his face as he looked down at me.

"God, Lex. You're seriously the most perfect, beautiful woman I have ever seen. I'm so fucking lucky, and I loved that you growled at me. So I might have to tease—" I grabbed his hair and pulled him close to my face. "Ouch! Okay, no teasing. My woman has needs," he said, but he was smiling and so was I.

I was so glad I'd let him in and given him a chance. He didn't just wear his heart on his sleeve, Ranger was a complicated guy. I was only at just the tip of the iceberg with him. He may have acted a certain way, but he deflected so much.

He kissed me, his hands going under my top as my hands went to his boxers. I rubbed his hard length through the thin material, and he moaned into my mouth.

"I won't last long if you do that, and this morning is about you." Pushing my T-shirt up, he kissed and licked my nipples, which were hard and needy. I watched as he kissed his way down, every so often stopping to look at me, watch me. When he got to the top of my wet folds, he took a deep inhale.

"God, you smell amazing," he said, but before I could answer, he licked and sucked on my clit. The pleasure snapped me like a rubber band, and I went flying over the edge into a blissful orgasm. He didn't stop, keeping the rhythm, his fingers joining in, and I clutched the sheets, needing something to keep me anchored to this world.

When I felt his fingers enter me, I knew I needed more. My core clenched around him, sucking him deeper as he flicked my clit over and over with the edge of his tongue, before he sucked again, his fingers finding that magic spot inside, stroking me into another orgasm.

"Oh fuck, Ranger. Holy shit." I grabbed a sheet and balled it up in my fist, turning my head and biting it so I stopped making so much noise. I didn't want everyone to hear us.

"You like that?" he asked, and the only answer I could give him was pushing his head back down. His chest rumbled with laughter, and I felt it through my body as he went back to sucking and fucking me with his fingers.

My body was covered in sweat, and I was so close, so sensitive. I gripped the back of his head and rode out the most incredible orgasm. I flopped onto the mattress and sunk down, half dazed, with a smile on my face.

"So, am I a keeper?" he asked out of nowhere. I laughed and rolled into him, inhaling his scent. His hard chest pressed against me as he hugged me tight.

"Yeah...for now." He kissed me and rubbed himself against my belly a couple of times. I reached my hand down, but he grabbed it before I could touch him.

"It was all about you this morning, you don't have to do that," he said. I cocked my brow but saw he was serious. He really was all about me, and as much as I loved that about him, I would love to watch him get off with my hands.

"I want to touch you, watch you come," I said as I ran my hand down his chest, feeling the dark hairs of that sexy trail leading down to the waistband on his boxers. My fingers inched their way under, grasping his hot, silky cock in my hand, and he hissed as I gave it a small stroke.

"Fuck, Lex. I usually last longer, it's just—" I stroked again, and his body shivered and bucked in my hand. I rubbed my thumb over the head, spreading the pre-cum glistening on top, and that was all it took to send him over the edge.

"Lexi, oh fuck." His hand flew down to mine, grasping it in his, and I watched as rope after rope of cum hit his belly, his forearm, my hand, and my T-shirt.

"Holy fuck, that was...fast. *Intense*," he said and

kissed me once, then twice before I felt the cum sticking my shirt to his belly and chuckled.

"I should get cleaned up. Did you want to have a shower with me? I'll wash your back if you wash mine," he said, wearing a cheeky grin, but a shower sounded nice.

Before I could answer, there was a loud knock on the door.

"You two, let's shower in separate rooms. Father isn't exactly happy. You guys need to sneak around better, or at least wait until he's out of the house and far away," Jett called from outside my door.

Ranger's eyes went wide at the news that Alaric had heard us. Fuck. I laid back, my clean hand going to my face. That was kinda embarrassing. If his dad heard us...fuck, everyone probably heard us.

"You weren't that loud, so don't worry. No one else heard," Ranger said, trying to comfort me, but even he didn't look convinced. There was a knock again, and the door opened. I pulled the sheets up and saw Jett standing at the doorway, grinning and shaking his head.

"Everyone heard... Next time, use Galen's place."

I groaned. "Stop with your super hearing shit. Turn it off."

Jett winked. "But I might miss something important if I do. Like you and my brother getting —" Ranger threw a pillow at him, and I laughed as Jett caught it.

I rolled over and hugged myself into Ranger.

"Douchebag," I called out once Jett left the room.

"Let's go have that shower." Ranger grabbed me around the waist and hauled me off the bed. I really needed to wash my hand.

CHAPTER 34
LEXI

I was so happy Josh had come to visit, I wasn't sure with the whole Russet pack threat and everything else going on that I would see him. But if they thought it was safe to have him here then I was going to have as much fun as I could with him.

"Check it out, it's got a snorkel." I showed him the goggles and snorkel I had bought while Ranger was blowing up my new yellow lounge chair. So I could float around on top while Josh looked for things under water in the shallow end. And wearing his floaties.

"I love it, Lexi. We can take turns." And he gave me a big hug, I reached down and hugged him back. God I loved this kid, he was too beautiful.

"I can teach you how to swim if you want?" Ranger offered, but Josh moved closer to me, he was still wary of him. I rubbed his back a few times.

"It's okay, Ranger is a good swimmer, if you want to learn he would be a great teacher." Well I hoped he would be, Josh finally stepped away from me and nodded, you could tell he was still nervous. He was considered an outsider too, he came from a different pack like Raff. But I thought he would feel more at home here in Kiba, he had Grayson and Jack and the pack. But everything isn't always that easy. I know.

"Joshua, I think that was such a nice offer by Ranger, if you learn to swim then I'm sure they will let you swim in the pool here more often." Jack spoke up from the chair he was sitting on nearby. That was encouraging, and Josh stood up straight.

"Yes please, Ranger." I could see the huge grin on Ranger's face. Like he had just won over the most important person in my life... and that would be true. Josh was my little brother, you didn't have to share the same blood to be siblings and I claimed him as mine. The other boys who lived with him, Jaxon and Harry, they were cousins. They were from the same pack, and always stuck together. Like they were now, they were off playing football with Grayson, they didn't want to get in the pool.

Ranger placed the lounger in the pool and helped me get onto it, at first I thought it silly him helping me, I could do it myself. Um... nope. That was a fail. It moved so fast on the water that I almost fell in. When

I was safely onboard, wearing once again a tank top and boyleg underwear because I forgot to buy myself swimwear when I went to Walmart... or maybe I just liked being a little more covered up? I started floating away from them and Josh waved to me, like I was going somewhere far away. I smiled and waved back. This day was turning out to be the warmest and I was grateful the weather had been so good.

"Okay Josh, I'm going to show you how to get out of the pool safely, how to float on your back and then we will move onto some more swimming techniques. But there are rules and you have to promise me, that you will never break them."

Josh's eyes were wide, nodding, taking in everything Ranger was telling him, shit I was taking in everything too. He was so... commanding. It was then you could tell he was the son of the alpha. Even though I thought he was the least like his father, maybe he was more like him than I first realized. But just not as intense and scary but he could hold his own.

"The biggest, number one rule of them all is... never ever get into a pool alone. You must always have an adult with you, and you have to ask permission. You can't jump in without their okay. You understand?"

Ranger stood up to his full height and looked down at Josh. I thought he was going to run away to

Jack the way he took a step backwards. But then he put his fists on his hips and nodded.

"Yes. I got it. What's rule two?" And then cheeky grin spread across Ranger's face as he squatted down to Josh's height, it had me gripping the sides of my floating lounger chair when Ranger turned to look at me with that glint in his eyes. *Oh boy.*

"We splash your big sister." Tears welled up in my eyes at what he had said, not the splashing, but he called me Josh's big sister and that hit me right in the feels. So bad. I tried to sit up and wipe my eyes without Josh seeing, but I didn't need to worry about that. Ranger had him on his hip and was now wading in the pool water towards me. The two of them stalking me then a huge wave of water hit me, I spluttered. Wiping water from my eyes, my hair was now wet and sticking to my face.

"Hey, that's not fair." I tried to splash them back and tease them back, but that was a fail. I splashed myself more than anyone. Jack was laughing now. Encouraging Josh to get me again and when he did it only hit my foot. But it was so cute with his cheeky grin and the light in his eyes because he splashed me.

"Ranger, get her." He was tapping on Ranger's chest, wanting him to splash me again, I was worried I would slip off this thing and into the deep end. I pointed my finger at the two of them, my grin just as wide.

"Don't. You. Dare."

That was all Ranger needed to hear, before he spun in a huge arc and a tidal wave of water came at me, but it was not as intense as before, it just rocked me around and had me screaming and holding on for life. Josh's giggles were all worth it though, and I laughed too. His giggles were infectious and I loved to hear them.

"Alright, we better leave your sister alone, or I will be in the bad books and sleeping in the wolf house. Let's get to work, and you will be swimming on your own in no time buddy. You got this and I got you."

Yep... Ranger was a keeper.

CHAPTER 35

LEXI

The last few days since Ranger and I fooled around in my bed and had fun in the pool with Josh had been filled with the guys on patrol. There was no more fooling around, football games or parties, just more and more men at the Lovells' house and a lot of howling, and it seemed to be an endless cycle. As much as they tried to shield me from it, I knew it was bad.

"Okay, give it to me straight. Pack Russet wants you back and they won't leave until you leave with them?" I wasn't dumb. Day in, day out, I always had one of them with me. Right now, Galen was in a meeting with Pack Bardoul, since they had come to help out, which worried me even more. Why would they want to help Raff and me?

"The pack, they don't want me. They want... you," The words tumbled out of Raff in a whisper.

Holy shit. This was what I worried about, and now it was happening. It had only been a week since Callum had bitten me and my blood healed Galen, making him strong, and now they wanted me.

"We won't let them have you, Lexi, but they're getting out of hand. Alaric didn't want us to scare you so we were ordered not to tell you. I've struggled with this for days, but you need to know. My uncles haven't come here for me. They want you, and they know what you are. It's bad."

My heart sank, as my hands shook. They wanted me for my blood, I had feared this... it was as if I could sense it coming and I knew that they would kill anyone in their way for it.

"I should go. Hide out somewhere—" Raff hugged me tight, cutting my words off, and I could feel him trembling. "I don't want them hurting anyone to get to me. I need you all safe."

Galen came in the room just at that moment. Well, I guessed it was his bedroom. We'd been staying here since the accidental overshare that Ranger and I provided the other morning. Alaric hadn't been able to look me in the eye for the rest of the day. But now I suspect it was this huge secret he wasn't telling me, and that was why he was avoiding me.

"We aren't running, Lexi, okay?" Galen said. "We will protect you. There's a meeting today between the other packs. Rawlins and Kenneally, they know what is happening and are going to help, but that means you won't be going back to school. Not for now at least. But you don't need to worry about classes or homework. I may have played with your records a little before spring break, so you will graduate."

My mouth dropped open. "You played with my record? Is that how I ended up in your history class to start off with?"

The sly grin on his lips told me that yes, he did. I shook my head and laughed.

"I can't believe you," I told him, but I could believe him. I wasn't upset. Actually, I was impressed. Plus I didn't have to go to school, and I would still graduate and everything, which sounded great to me. If only we could get rid of these assholes who wanted to kidnap me, then everything could go back to the way it was before. Right?

"Look, why don't we have a little bit of fun today? Mav is off duty after one, and we could invite Ada over and swim a little, while the weather is nice," Galen rubbed my arm as he kissed my forehead, and I grabbed his sweater before he could leave.

"What about you?" I asked, but he shook his head. I wondered if he didn't want anyone seeing his body, the scars. I hadn't even seen it, not all of it at least. And I wouldn't push him, I told him that I wouldn't. But I wanted him to still have fun, he could wear a t-shirt... a long sleeve one.

"No, I have to work. I need to be involved in the meeting between the packs," he looked tired and worn out, so I nodded. I didn't want to push him when he already had so much on his plate. He did work for Kiba, so it made sense that he would need to attend the meeting.

I curled into a ball, and Raff held me tight. All I could hear were the sounds of our breathing and the beat of our hearts. It was like the calm before the storm. And I needed this, just laying here. Doing nothing, not having something to do. The sunlight was streaming through cracks in the curtain and it was just perfect. The small dust motes dancing in the golden stream.

I let out a deep breath, and snaked my hand under Raff's T-shirt to his abs. I pressed my palm against his warm skin. Just needing a little more skin contact. I tickled his happy trail of hair and he chuckled a little and kissed my head. I realized he needed this just as much as me. I closed my eyes, and started dreaming about what the future held for me.

CHAPTER 36
LEXI

Ada wrapped her arms around me as our feet dangled in the pool. We were watching Maverick and Saint doing laps, play fighting, and just having fun. It was nice to see the guys in the pool, relaxing, just being free. I still didn't have any swim wear. It wasn't safe to go out shopping, so I was back in the tank and boylegs. Not that any of the guys had complained.

Ada on the other hand, she was wearing a red bikini, and she looked hot. Oh, yeah she was nervous as hell when she showed me, but I told her she needs to go out there, show all of them how confident she was. Saint did a double take when he saw her. Actually, he stumbled into the pool and tried to cover it up like he was diving in, but I saw. So did Maverick and he just smiled while shaking his head. I almost wanted to push them to be in the same room together... alone. Play cupid, I knew she liked him. And he must like her... they just needed a push, in the right direction.

"That's so bullshit you don't have to go to school, but only 'cause I would miss you. I wonder if Galen would do that for my grades, then I can come hang out with you all day?" Ada said and I smiled. Maybe he could.

Maverick overheard—more like always listening — and swam up to me, pulling on my legs, and I braced myself on his shoulders.

"He won't do it for us," he told Ada. "Plus, he isn't working at the school any longer." Maverick pulled again and dragged me into the pool's cool water.

"He quit?" I asked, but instead of answering, he planted his lips on mine and spun me around. The water splashed up at Ada, who just watched us with a smile on her face. I could see it in her eyes, she was happy for me. She wanted something like this too, and I really hoped I could maybe help make it happen.

"Can't be dating a student. That's a big no no," Saint said as he swam past us and over to Ada, I could see her starting to blush from his attention. "Let's have fun and not think about this bad shit for a while. Come and get on my shoulders, Ada. Lexi, you jump up on Maverick's shoulders. We are gonna play."

I saw Ada's eyes light up at that, and she didn't need to be told twice. She wrapped her legs over Saint's shoulders and held his head for balance as he made his way into the deep end. Maverick let go of me and dropped under the water. I let out a little squeal when his head came up between my legs and he pushed me up, my legs dangling over his shoulders my hands grabbing his dark hair for balance as he lifted me up in the air.

"Could have warned me," I teased. He grabbed my hands and lowered them down his chest, my breasts pressing into his head. He took that moment to shake his head, the water droplets spraying my face as he walked down to the side opposite to Saint and Ada.

"We got this. We'll be champions by the end of the day," Ada cheered, then smirked as she patted Saint's head, and I laughed. She was enjoying this, and it made me feel a little giddy inside, I wanted to play matchmaker so bad, but I think it was working itself out without me.

"Oh, you think you'll be?" I taunted teasingly. "Bring it on."

She put her fists up in front of her, then moved them to her waist as she wobbled slightly. "It has already been brought."

Then we just peeled into laughter, and the guys had no idea why we were laughing at that, he needed to check out more chick flicks with us. They moved closer to each other, and we giggled and laughed as we wrestled each other. I tried to push Ada off, but Saint held her tight. Maverick wasn't letting go either, and we just ended up high fiving each other.

"I know. How about you swim with us on your backs, and we'll see which one is faster?" I suggested.

The guys thought that was a great idea, and it didn't take long to be flipped over on Maverick's back with my arms wrapped around his neck. I watched as Saint did the same with Ada. I looked over to her and winked, and she smiled as she plastered her front to his back and mouthed, "We are just friends." *Yeah, yeah...you tell yourself that.* I knew better.

"One, two, thr—" I felt the muscles in Maverick's shoulders flex as he dove down under the water and I went with him. I wasn't ready and held my breath a little too late as he raced through the water, and when he came up and tapped the end, Saint and Ada were right beside us.

I coughed. I may have drunk a little of the pool.

"Shit, Lexi are you alright?" Maverick sounded worried as he held my hands. I nodded, then shook my head no.

"I didn't think you were going to take me under the water. I thought I was going to ride you like a dolphin or something." I could see he was concerned. He knew I couldn't swim, even though he did try and teach me earlier, it was sweet that he tried. But I decided swimming lessons were best for another day. I wanted to have fun, not half drown the whole time.

"I didn't even think about it. I've never had someone ride my back before."

Saint laughed and said, "Hey, that's not true. Alaric is always riding yours."

Maverick turned and splashed water at him. "He rides everyone's backs. He's the alpha, that's his job." Maverick turned back to me, his hand ran down my cheek and he kissed me briefly. "Do you want to go again?"

I shrugged and looked over to Ada who was behind Saint nodding her head at me, her eye wide pleading me to say yes. Yeah...just friends, my *ass*.

"Best of three?" I challenged.

CHAPTER 37
LEXI

It was weird spending the day without the guys. It was the first day back, and they had all left for school and I was here, alone. As alone as one could be with so many shifters surrounding the house to protect me. I had my phone with me and the chat was blowing up, mostly Ranger. Telling me every little thing he was doing as if I wanted to know when he was taking a crap. Yes, he told me he was going to take a shit then go to English. Um... who writes that to their girlfriend. I didn't need to know *everything.*

Galen really had quit, he told me he did it after the Callum thing, and I didn't know. He didn't want to tell me, so I spent the whole of spring break worried I was making out with my teacher. Who was actually not my teacher anymore.

He was working in Alaric's office with some of

the other alphas. Apparently, there was a breach last night, and a vampire had gotten through and close to the house before they could take him down. I didn't ask what that meant, like did they bite him with their venom? Was he going to die? Or did they escort him off the Kiba territory.

I hadn't been able to shake the feeling that something big was going to happen, and soon. Like this was my power, I could sense a war coming.

"Don't worry Lex, we got you," Jett said, I turned to him and glared, when he stuck his tongue out I slapped him across the arm.

"You can't call me Lex. I barely let Ranger call me that."

I heard a deep rumble and saw a very attractive guy standing just inside the kitchen. He had long, jet-black hair that was tied up into a messy bun, his skin was a few shades darker than Jett's, and he had the most beautiful eyes. Fuck, how the hell did Clare leave these two?

"Mekhi?" Like I had to ask. He held out his hand to me, and I walked over and took it. It was rough with calluses, but he gave me a firm hand shake.

"Glad to finally meet you. If ass here is giving you any trouble, just let me know and I'll kick it," he said, and I chuckled when Jett protested, holding his hands up in defense.

"He is a bit of an ass at times, but I'll let you know if I need help kicking his."

There was a bit of an awkward silence between the three of us, and I wasn't too sure if it was me or the situation. But then I saw their eyes had darted to the side. They must be hearing something. Fuck, I wish I could hear like they did.

"Let's get you some food, because Princess *Lexi* likes to eat, and we will set you up with your Kindle. Or you can come play some *Fortnite* with us. Either way, you have us until your mates get home from school, or Galen is finished doing whatever it is they're doing in there."

Food, reading...and watching to see if Mekhi and Jett were more than friends? Yep, sign me up for that. I had no idea what *Fortnite* was, so I didn't know if I wanted to play it.

AND YEP, I didn't want to play it. I gave it a go, and Jett laughed so hard, I couldn't walk and shoot. It was so hard and they tried so hard to give me tips but after shooting at the sky instead of the person I was supposed to and I died, I gave up. That game was not in my skillset, I turned back to my Kindle. It was hard to concentrate with them yelling and shooting people, but I didn't mind too much. It was fun to watch them interact. I could tell Mekhi kept Jett's toes on the ground, and the two of them balanced each other in such a beautiful way. Even when they were playing together, it was fun watching them.

Jett's character died, and he started eating popcorn. They were both facing the TV, and he was feeding Mekhi while he was still playing. It was cute, like they were an old married couple.

I was re-reading Cali Mann's academy series, snuggled up with a cupcake that Grayson had brought over for me yesterday. He'd brought a whole heap, and I'd called dibs on them but totally ate too many. I had a belly ache, but I didn't care... His cakes were the best.

"You gonna let me eat some?"

I looked up, and Jett was perched beside me, so I grabbed the cupcake and pulled it to my chest before he could grab it.

"Hell no. You'll make it out like it was more than just cake to Ranger and fuck with his head. You know he doesn't like you eating my *cake*."

Mekhi laughed as he put the controller down.

"Can I have some cake?"

I sat up a little straighter. What the hell was happening? Did he know what he was asking, or did he just really want cake?

"Oh man, you so want some of Lexi's cake. And tell Ranger how good it was," Jett teased, my mouth dropped open.

"Jett, shut up. No cake. There is only cake for

me," I said. The two of them laughed as Jett threw popcorn at Mekhi and he caught it in his mouth.

"I'm just messing around," Mekhi said. "I know what the cake thing is, and honestly, Ranger deserves it. You know he used to flirt non-stop with Clare? He was everywhere she was, and it drove us mad. So it's fun to give it to him a little. Plus, he has almost no control over his wolf, so that's just asking to be teased."

I sucked in a breath.

"So he would flirt with her, and you just let him?" I asked.

Jett settled in beside me, his arm over the back of the chair. "Well, we didn't let him. You know how hard it is to tell Ranger no. But after our mom died...I kinda took him under my wing. My father was not great at that time, and he already had enough on his plate. Maverick went the other way, he became quiet, reserved, didn't want to talk about it. He spent more time with Lyell."

This was the first time I was really hearing about their mom. There were photos, and I'd seen that she was beautiful, but no one ever mentioned her.

"Is it rude to ask how she died?" I wasn't sure if Jett wanted to talk about it, but from what I'd gathered, it happened about five or six years ago. I was curious, but I didn't want to push for the story.

Jett settled deeper into the chair beside me, his

hand touching my shoulder just lightly. He cleared his throat, and said, "Father is in his office, so I can talk about it a bit. He won't hear me. He doesn't like anyone talking about it. Okay?" he said in warning. I nodded as I glanced at him, but his eyes were focused on the screen and I could tell he wasn't really watching at it.

"I was thirteen, and the pack was having issues with some vampires. They weren't good, not like Galen. They killed innocent people in and around Port Willow, and my father and the other alphas couldn't stand for it. We value all lives, not just that of our pack. But pack comes first.

"There was a fight, and the packs killed one of them. What my father didn't know was that one of them was a day walker, like Galen. When he was out with the other alphas and we were all at school, they broke in, attacked and killed my mother." Jett took a deep breath, and I could tell it was hard to talk about. Hell, I didn't even talk about my mom or the man I thought was my dad.

"Alaric painted the whole house white after that, so there were no dark corners to hide in." Mekhi added.

My heart sank. That was why the house was so white, so clinical. So you would see a vampire standing there, ready to attack you. I reached over and hugged Jett. God, that was horrible. At least my mother had died quickly. I didn't want to think of what his mom went through.

"My mom was killed too. I understand how hard that is, and I will always be here for you if you want to talk about it."

He hugged me back, but the tension was still there. I wanted to lighten the mood a little after such a tragic story, so I asked them.

"Do you guys want a cupcake?"

CHAPTER 38

LEXI

I tried out *Fortnite* one more time before Jett put some music on and we danced around the room. It was nice...freeing really. We laughed a lot, and pretended that everything was good and there weren't a bunch of rogue shifters and vampires out for my blood.

I tried out the ants power on Jett, and it was the best five minutes, watching him dance around like they were tickling his skin. Mekhi and I just laughed and rolled around on the floor as we watched Jett, my stomach hurting from laughing so much. But as for my angel power, it kinda sucked. And we ate all the cupcakes.

Eventually, Galen came for me. He was going to take me back for lunch, but ended up staying with us. He tried a hand at *Fortnite*, and he was so much better at it than me. So Jett and Galen played a few rounds, while Mekhi and I watched and ate Doritos. Before I knew it, the guys were back, and it didn't sound like it was good.

"We had word that there is a band of rogue shifters, along with Pack Russet and night vamps coming here. They have joined together as one group to attack us, and so we need to be prepared. They are coming to start a war, but we will end it," Alaric said to the gathered crowd. Everyone was out on the front lawn of the Lovell's. I noticed a lot of the guys I didn't like from the other packs, like Parker Tolson. He was an asshole, and he was eying me in a way that made my skin crawl. Made me want to use my ant power on him, but I would have to touch him and I wasn't going to do that.

"We will set the women and children up inside," Alaric continued. "For the rest of you, we will prepare for a fight. It might come tonight, but there is a full moon tomorrow, and I believe they are waiting until then. Either way...we will be ready."

There were a lot of fists pumping in the air, and cheers, growls and a few howls. They knew what they were doing, but I felt like a total asshole for bringing this to them. I didn't ask to be born a half angel, or however much I had in me. I didn't mean to heal Galen, I didn't want Callum biting me, and I sure as hell didn't want to be kidnapped by a bunch of scary wolves, panthers, bears, and whatever else was out there. They told me it a was a mix of shifters.

I couldn't even be happy with death, because I knew they wouldn't kill me. They needed me alive to get what they wanted over and over. I was glad in that moment that I didn't have any family left outside these gates that they could use against me. Grayson and Jack were here with the boys. They were safe—

"Ada," I gasped. She wasn't here. She needed to be here, safe in the walls with the pack's protection. Ranger pulled me closer to his side as Maverick smoothed my hair and kissed the top of my head.

"She'll be fine," Ranger said. "Don't worry about her. They're only after you, Lex."

Raff moved forward and right into my face. He didn't blink, he just stared, his blue eyes swirling. "No, Lexi is right," he said. "Ada is too important to her for them not to use her. We need to get her parents somewhere safe too. They'll be coming for her. Lexi wouldn't let anything happen to them, and they know that. She needs to be here."

Galen cupped Raff's shoulder before he said, "I'm on it." Then he ran off towards Alaric.

I felt safe with my mates' arms around me. I saw some of the women with their mates and felt as if they were all staring at me. I was the reason this was happening. But when kind eyes landed on me, I knew I had to speak to her. Her long blonde hair was in a messy bun on top of her head, and she had two of her big mates standing beside her while the other two were standing further back, talking to some other men.

"I just need to talk to someone. Can you wait here?" I asked as I pulled away, but Maverick surprised me when he didn't let go. He was a little clingier today, and I understood his fear, but I just needed a few minutes.

"I'll be fine. I'm just going over there." I gestured to where Noah's mom was, still watching me. I just... I needed to rip off this band-aid. I wanted to apologize for coming in and turning their life upside down. Maverick quickly hugged me, then turned and walked away towards Saint.

I took a deep breath and made my way over. I noticed the tall guys both wore similar expressions. Were they brothers too? They smiled down at me. They were as big as Noah, and I had to assume one of them was his biological father. I wondered if they knew who the biological father was when there were so many mates. Oh too many thoughts.

"Hello, Alexis. I'm Zara." She had blue eyes, and you could tell she was just one of those really nice moms, the type who would cut the crusts off your sandwiches and make funny faces out of pancakes.

"I...I wanted to say that I'm sorry for everything

that's happened. I never meant for any of this, or what happened with Callum. I just..." I could feel the tears coming. Her son was gone because of me, and she wouldn't see or hear from him again...maybe ever. She gave me a sad smile and embraced me. She was soft and warm, and it was easy to hug her back. She smelled so nice, and she stroked my hair and told me it was okay, that I shouldn't be sorry.

"I'm so glad you came over. I've wanted to meet you for such a long time," she said, and I was surprised. I didn't think she would want to meet me, and she must've been able to tell I was thinking that.

"You're the young woman that sent a bunch of teenage boys crazy. I wanted to meet you and help you learn how to handle more than one mate, but I can see that you're doing just fine with the Lovell twins, that red wolf and Galen. You surprised even me when you picked the vampire, which meant I wanted to meet you even more. You must be a strong woman," Zara said as she held my hands in hers. Why was she being so nice? She wasn't even mad at me.

"I'm sorry that my son hurt you. What he did, I could never forgive, but he's always been a hot head. My Noah, he thinks the world of you, and he is smitten with your friend, Ada. It's all we hear about. I think his fathers are about to tape his mouth shut if he doesn't stop, and even Elijah has been avoiding coming home."

I bit my lip, trying to hide my smile. I didn't think Noah would like me knowing this, but then, it was really cute when she said he was smitten. Ada would freak if she heard this, but I kinda wanted her and Noah to get together too. Of course I was shipping them, he was smitten.

"But we have lots of time to get to know each other. If you have any questions about having four mates, I'm happy to help. It can be challenging at times, and I was once like you. Until I met four handsome men who swept me off my feet."

Big hands wrapped around her and lifted her in the air. "Did I just hear you have a handsome mate? You better be talking about me." Her laugh was infectious, and I laughed too. He kissed her, then planted her feet back on the ground.

"Hi, Alexis. I'm James. The boys have told me so much about you. Welcome to the pack, darling." His hand stretched out for me to shake, so I smiled and took it. This wasn't what I was expecting. I'd thought they were going to yell at me, tell me it was all my fault for not picking Callum as a mate. I hadn't understood the whole dynamic before, but I did now. Packmate bonds were really strong, and I'd messed that up, took that away from Callum, and caused all of this.

CHAPTER 39
MAVERICK

The wind swirled around me as I stood watch. It was dark out and had started to rain a little, but I could see for miles and didn't care about getting wet, this was important. All that mattered was protecting my mate, my pack. Saint was with me, and all of us went out in groups of two. I was going to ask for Ranger and Raff to be with me, but Father said it would be best to separate us, only because we were so strongly bound to Lexi that we might not wait for back-up.

He was worried we would get ourselves killed and that we would understand when the time came. The need to protect one's mate was the strongest feeling in the world, and our wolf would do anything for Lexi.

So the two of us sat there, side by side, listening...waiting and watching for the threats. I would wait here every night for the rest of my life if it meant Lexi was safe.

I HAD BEEN THINKING a lot about a commitment ceremony, our way of getting married. It usually involved the female being bitten and turned into a shifter. That wasn't going to happen with Lexi, and I was so grateful, but I still wanted that—the vows, declaring ourselves in front of the whole pack.

It would tie me to Galen even more so, and after that kiss... I couldn't believe I was the one to make that move, it was like a huge weight had been lifted from my shoulders. I hadn't told Ranger, something I'd have thought I would've done. But I think he knew from the looks on our faces.

I mostly kept it to myself, but I did tell one person who I knew wouldn't judge me—Saint. He'd slapped my back and said, "Finally. I knew you had a huge crush on him. Good for you." That was all I'd needed to end the torment within myself. I had a beautiful mate, and I'd kissed the guy I had been crushing on for as long as I could remember. I was the black sheep of my family...well, it was either me or Lyell, but having a crush on your male, vampire history teacher set the bar pretty high for things my father wouldn't like. And the only thing my father would have had a problem with was the vampire part. If Galen was human he wouldn't have cared, he would have encouraged it in fact.

If it wasn't for Lexi, I would never have told him. I'd still be stuck in limbo, not knowing who I was or where I was going. I was so glad that she didn't listen to me when I told her to leave Kiba, that she dug her heels in and basically told me to fuck myself.

Fuck, Lexi really was one of a kind. I hoped Saint got to experience that one day.

THE RAIN PICKED UP, making it harder to see, and it was messing with my hearing. I made a low whining sound, letting Saint know I was struggling with this change of weather. He made a few low growls in agreement. That was when I heard the first warning howl, and it was chilling. I felt it through my bones. Then the sounds of loud growls and injured wolves, but I didn't know if it was theirs or ours. We heard the howling call for back-up. Saint and I were straight to our feet, racing along the trail to where the fight was taking place. The ground slipping beneath us, rain making the dirt turn to mud, making it harder to get to them.

The scene in front of me started to become clear. A large grey wolf was on the ground, his body twisted in a heap, red blood pouring from a wound on his neck. He would heal, I didn't know who he was, but he would heal, he was a shifter. He wasn't a Kiba wolf but he was on our side. The larger wolf was trying to hold back three red wolves and a vampire. Fuck. He had a lot of damage already to his flank and he was favoring his front left paw.

My wolf's vision narrowed, and I felt almost disconnected from body as pure instinct took over. I lunged at the nearest wolf, his reaction slow as I bit into his flesh, ripping at his throat, the taste of tainted blood on my tongue. They were on drugs, which seemed their reaction time was a little slower. The vamp though, he wasn't. I dodged his mouth as he tried to sink his teeth into me. Fuck, I have never been in this situation before, but was glad for all the times I messed with my brothers and avoiding their teeth.

I'd never used my venom before, but it was now dripping from my fangs. I could taste it, and it stirred an even deeper feeling in me. I bared my teeth, warning them to leave. But I wanted them to fight me, so I could have the chance to kill these shifters. I wanted to make them pay for all they did to Rafferty, my packmate. They never deserved Raff, and he was mine now. He was my family.

I bit into the wolf again this time letting my

venom enter his system, but he twisted and I lost my hold on him as he caught my hind leg between his teeth. Crunching down hard, I felt his venom running through the wound. I poured everything I had into fighting him off and twisted beneath him. He wasn't anticipating the move and let go as I sank my teeth into his belly. He howled out in pain as I pulled and ripped until I was covered in his blood and the others were retreating, tails between their legs, their vampire friend long gone. Their loyalty was nothing like that of a real pack.

I heard the whimper from Saint, and it drew my vision back to the scene in front of me. I couldn't stop my body from trembling as the cold rain, the loss of blood, the venom hitting me all at once. I saw the wolf was still there, lying on his side, unmoving.

"Shit, I think he's dying. Help me, please," a dark figure said from beside him, his hands running through the wolf's blood-soaked fur. It was Caleb, he was a few years older than me from Pack Kenneally.

Saint shifted back and said, "Fuck, how come he isn't healing?"

Where was everyone? Why didn't anyone else come to help? I let out a long painful howl, but it went unanswered.

"Run back, tell them we're coming. We'll carry him." Saint called over to me.

My leg protested a little, as it hadn't finished

healing from the break, but I didn't slow down. I pushed harder, letting out warning howl that we were on our way. It was answered by a female wolf from the house. Where was everyone else?

———

WHEN I ARRIVED, there was two female wolves standing by the door to the kitchen. I shifted, "We need help. They're bringing one of our wolves back, but he isn't healing." It was then I saw Lexi, standing just off to the side with Ada, her eyes wide and glassy. Ada let out a small gasp. I didn't want her to see this, I wanted to shield her from it all.

"They're testing us now, pressing on our defenses. Everyone else is out fighting, bring him to us. We'll help him. Who is it?" one of the women questioned, and I looked back at her, recognizing she was someone's mother, but I wasn't sure whose. I felt guilty not knowing who it was that had been injured protecting Lexi. But they were in wolf form

"Pack Rawlins," I replied and lowered my head, seeing my body for the first time. My leg had all but healed, but the rain and blood had mixed, and ran like small rivers all down my body and causing the white tiles below my feet to turn pink.

It didn't stop Lexi though. Her body enveloped mine, and I wrapped her in my arms, trembling. My wolf was on edge, but was relieved to feel his mate in his arms.

Father was right—I couldn't control him. When a threat was there in front of me, he took over to protect what was mine.

And Lexi was mine.

CHAPTER 40
LEXI

Maverick was standing there, naked, soaked with rain and blood. So much blood, it turned the floor pink beneath his feet. I let out a sob. I couldn't believe this was really happening, but the vision of Maverick was all I needed as proof that it was. Alaric had said they wouldn't fight tonight, that the full moon was tomorrow and he expected them to go to war then. This was a nightmare, and I had lived through enough of them to know this one was the biggest of them all.

"Get blankets and towels. Bottles of water, warm water, and bandages," one of the older ladies called out. There was a flurry of movement around me from the other women, Ada among them. She had told me she couldn't believe this was happening, but wanted to help in any way she could. She didn't want to be up the top with the children, neither did I. She was ready to put everything on the line and fight with us. For me. She was the most amazing friend I had ever had. But it was my time to protect her, and I wouldn't let anything happen to her.

The dining table was cleared and a blanket laid down as the women called out that the wolf was arriving.

"Quick bring him here," someone called out as Saint and a guy I didn't know carried a huge wolf inside and placed him gently on the table in front of us.

It was then I heard a woman sob, her hand reaching out to the still wolf as she said, "Hux, oh god, baby."

Ada was there at Saint's side, holding up a towel for him, and a bottle of water. Maverick stood back, a towel now wrapped around his waist as he watched the women tending to the lifeless wolf.

"How come he isn't healing?" someone voice shrieked.

"I don't understand?" Another questioned.

They looked so lost as they ran their hands over his wet fur, covered in blood, twigs, and dirt.

"Hux, baby. Wake up. God, please wake up," a woman I assumed was his mother said. She had her hands on his face, trying to open his eyes. Her cry's breaking something inside me. How could this happen. I had to help him, save him like I did with

Galen, but I didn't know how. Did I give him my blood? He wasn't a vampire.

I felt a pull to the dying wolf, my body stepping closer on it own accord, as I felt a warm sensation in my hand. I looked down, but nothing was there. It was if I could only sense it not see it. I stepped closer again, until I was beside the poor women sobbing over the wolf. Hux...Huxley Moore? Oh God, I had only just seen him last week at Walmart, I liked him, he was the only one not to sniff me at school.

She didn't push me away when I placed my hand, full of warmth on his head. It was if my body knew what to do, even though I had no idea what was happening. I only knew that Huxley was dying right in front of me and I needed to help him.

My breath left my lungs as I felt the pain, so much pain. I gasped as I took it in. I felt Maverick behind me, holding me tight. He was speaking, but it was like he was underwater. I only felt Huxley, all his injuries, and my hands wandered his fur until I found the cause of all his pain.

I uncovered a crescent shape, and the women around me gasped loudly. They started screaming and calling out to get Galen, but I placed my palm over the wound, I needed too. I wanted him to heal. At first, the pain was nothing compared to the pain I felt moments later. Then my body went ridged, I didn't scream or flinch. I wanted to let go so badly but I knew I couldn't until it was done. It felt like an eternity before the pain disappeared and I collapsed, Maverick catching me before I hit the ground.

As my hearing returned, I looked up the table, and all eyes were on Huxley. The women's eyes were red and filled with tears, shock and awe. They looked to me and then to where the wound was now healed

"Hux, oh god. My baby, shift back. Shift so we can help you, love."

I looked over to see Ada, her hands flew to her mouth, then she turned to grab another towel and rushed to the table. Maverick helped me to stand, and I saw him. Hux, he was shivering, curled into himself, his body covered in blood, but his dark brown eyes found mine. He looked back to who I believed was his mother, and she stroked his dark wet curls from his forehead.

"Huxley, how do you feel?" He let out a croak, and Ada was there in a flash, holding a bottle of water for him. He took it from her and downed it fast, I wasn't sure if that was a good idea to drink that fast or not, but he didn't seem to be sick from it. Ada placed another towel on him, then started running around and grabbing other supplies while the women took a step back, not understanding what had just happened.

Hell, I didn't even know what had just happened. I thought I healed him. No...I did heal him. I could still feel the pain lingering in my bones, it was the same pain I'd experienced when Callum bit me.

"Better, I don't hurt anymore," he said as he looked at me, he held my gaze.

Everyone now watched me, and I didn't like the attention and I wasn't sure what they were going to say. But when Huxley's mom wrapped her arms around me, thanking me for saving her son over and over, I realized maybe this power I had was meant for healing. Not to hurt others or stop a vampire or shifter, but to heal others from them.

Like how I could heat up Galen's arm. He was cold and a normal person was warm, so I must've helped him. The tingling ant feeling I gave them all... Okay, I didn't have an answer to that one. But I guessed that was why I couldn't make them cold.

I looked down at my hands and back to Huxley. He smiled and mouthed "Thank you," before his mother was back to smothering him while he tried to bat her away. Ada seemed to really be a natural in her role as caregiver, and after what I just saw, I thought she'd make a great nurse.

Saint hovered behind her, watching her every move as she touched Huxley. She tried to dry him with a towel, but Saint took the towel away and handed it to another woman. He turned Ada to him, I didn't know what was happening, was Saint injured still?

He pulled his towel from his waist and gave it to

her, dipping his wet hair down to her. She hesitated and looked around the room, her eyes caught mine and her brows went up in confusion. What... she then put the towel on his head and dried his hair, smiling the whole time. Oh, jealous much, Maverick's chest rumbled with a small chuckle, I let out a small laugh at the sight, and everyone turned to me.

Galen thankfully came in just then, his hands going to my face, my arms, checking me out before looking over to Huxley. "Are you alright, what happened. Did they reach here?" Too many questions, too fast.

"Galen...shhh," Maverick's voice was smooth and soft, and I loved feeling the words through his chest when he spoke, his voice deep and sexy. Everyone in the room placed their fingers on their lips. We wouldn't speak about this here, since it wasn't safe. And now I had a whole new skill set. I knew Galen didn't realize what had happened here was me, my power until now.

I felt drained and a little light headed. That was a lot to take in, I took in all Huxley's pain. Last time that happened I passed out.

"I need to sleep," I mumbled and felt Maverick scoop me up into his arms, resting me against his chest.

"Let's get you some water and somewhere to lay down, but best if you don't sleep." I felt Galen's hand smooth over my brow and smiled a little using all the strength I had not to fall asleep from his light touch.

"That makes me sleepy... keep doing it." Galen's fingers left my face and he pried open an eye. I groaned at the light. There was nothing wrong with a nap to recharge. I just needed to be ready again incase more are injured.

"Don't sleep." Galen hissed at me, I opened my other eye and saw his two dark ones look down at me. His fangs poking out through his lips.

"Oh, well if you're going to look like that, I will stay awake." His face pulled away slightly and I could feel Maverick chuckling again.

"I agree with Lexi, I would stay awake for that look." Galen just shook his head and gave us both a dazzling smile as he went off in search of some water.

Maverick laid me down against his chest as he settled just away from all the commotion.

"He is pretty hot when he goes full vamp, hey?" He looked down at me and I winked back up at him.

"Lexi, Lexi... what am I going to do with you?" he teased, his eyes looked troubled but he was putting on a brave face. For me. For everyone here.

"Kiss me?" I replied. Then I remembered he was fighting out there... biting other wolves, "on second thought... how about a raincheck on that kiss."

CHAPTER 41
LEXI

I woke up in Maverick's room. I was wearing his sweats and tee, and the light was filtering in through the small slit in the curtains. Ugh, too bright.

"Hey, sleeping beauty," Ada announced loudly in a perky voice which was just too much for first thing in the morning. As she came out of the bathroom, a towel around her head, dressed in a lovely sundress. I glanced around and saw that no one was in bed with me, but the sheets were all messed up, so they must have been here at one point.

"They're all good, just in a meeting. There are like, so many meetings today." She jumped up on the bed beside me and took my hand. "How are you feeling? Did you want some water?"

My throat felt dry, and I honestly felt like I'd spent the night doing shots and was paying for it now. My head even throbbed. One of those headaches? Yeah, they were back but not as bad as the first one, this was more like a dull ache behind my eyes.

"Yeah, I feel pretty shit," I rasped. She ran out of the room, then back again, unscrewing the lid of a water bottle before handing it to me. The water was cool and refreshing.

"Thanks, how is..." I didn't want to say too much, just incase it was being kept a secret. I know my healing him was being kept a huge secret and so many people knew about it. But when she flopped down beside me, her hand flew up and landed behind her I wasn't sure what that meant. I turned to Ada, her face beamed. This huge smile and glow in her cheeks.

"Oh god, yeah, he's doing great. Like... really, really great. He was up this morning and having breakfast, and said he wanted to come see you, but I said you weren't ready yet," she said, and my brows furrowed. Huh? When did Ada wake up, or go to bed?

"You just saw him?" I asked, and she tilted her head from side to side then nodded as she glanced back to the door.

"He's across the hall in Ranger's room. The other rooms were full, and Ranger gave his room to Pack Rawlins to rest in." She came in real close and whispered, "Most of them are in wolf form. There are so many, and they're all so pretty. Do you know how hard it is not to pet them all?" I leaned back into the pillow and smiled at Ada, thankful I mentioned the petting thing too her.

"So, you just went in there... right now?" Her eyes widened, as she reached the towel on her head and I laughed. She took it off and flicked the damp strands around. She looked so red now, someone was a little embarrassed. Which reminded me...

"So what was up with you and Saint last night?" I asked, wiggling my brows at her and she just rolled her eyes, but a smirk formed on her lips. Oh yeah, something was going on.

"I have no idea. He went all...caveman?" she said, throwing her hands up and laughed. I laughed too, because yes, he'd been a total caveman. He basically marked her right there in front of everyone when he took the towel, she was drying Huxley with and tossed it to someone else, then took the one he was wearing and asking her to dry his hair? Which was so weird.

There was knocking at the door, and Ada jumped up and skipped over to open it.

"I brought up some food?" The voice was female, and I could sense she seemed a little unsure.

"Come on in, Hazel, meet my best friend, Lexi," Ada held her arm open inviting this Hazel into the room.

A bright smile appeared at first, then dark brown

eyes found me and her smile widened. She had blonde hair nestled on top of her head in a messy bun and had to be in her late twenties.

"Hi, it's so nice to meet you. I'm here with Ben, Galen's friend. He's currently stuck inside Galen's basement." She smiled and shrugged. "I guess that's what happens when you date a vampire who can only come out at night."

Oh... shit. Ben, Galen had told me a little about him. How my blood had healed him. He just gave a little to him, to see if it could after pack Russet had bitten him with their venom. While he was protecting his girlfriend from them. I wasn't upset with Galen for not telling me, I was grateful that my blood could do that for him. Especially that he was protecting Hazel against Raff's dirty, rotten uncles.

SHE CLEARED HER THROAT. "I was told I could come here and help out and...I don't know. I'd love to make a friend who's also dating a vampire. Until this morning, I didn't know any other women who had a vampire boyfriend. And I guess really, two weeks ago, I didn't even know they existed."

She placed a tray full of fruit and pancakes beside me, then pulled a chocolate bar from her pocket and handed it to me, I took it without question, and she smiled.

"Okay, you brought me chocolate, we can be friends."

Ada laughed. "Wow, if that was all it took to be your friend, I should have started with that." I laughed too.

"Hey, you helped out Ranger with the whole chocolate buying idea. And you didn't have to work hard to be my friend. Did you?" I wasn't too sure now if I was a terrible friend or not. I wasn't the best at the whole thing but I was getting better.

"I'm only joking, Lexi. You were easy to stalk and force into being my friend."

It FELT GOOD, just talking like we were just three regular women, and nothing bad was going on... just for a minute at least. We spent the morning in bed, eating, hanging out, and talking about boys and boy problems. Pretty sure every wolf in the house could hear us, But there were hundreds of conversations going on, so they would've had to try really hard to overhear us. If they wanted too. Honestly I thought it would be boring for them to want to listen to us and our weird ramblings.

"I'm just gonna go check on Hux. I'll be back in a minute," Ada said, rolling off the bed and running into the bathroom. I looked to Hazel who also noticed and she smiled that knowing smile.

"Um...Ada, the door is that way," I called out,

and I could hear her clicking something open, as she mumbled something to herself.

"Yeah, I know. Just...gotta...do something. *Okay*?"

When she came out, I could see she had put on some eye makeup, and her blonde hair was brushed and curled to perfection.

"We won't wait up," I teased her. She turned and stuck her tongue out at me as she walked out the door, I laughed. Looked like someone had a crush on Hux... I hoped Noah or Saint didn't find out. Actually, pretty sure Saint worked that out last night with his caveman stunt.

Once Ada was gone, Hazel got really serious.

"How do you like, share the time between all of them?" she asked. She was still having trouble wrapping her head around the fact that I had four mates. And to be honest, I'd been feeling like that was something I was struggling with. Sharing was hard but must be harder on them as they all have to share me.

"Huh... Actually, it's hard...but thinking about it now, they make it easy when they pair off. Ranger and Raff...Galen and Maverick. Huh, I only just realized that now."

I couldn't really help and compare notes with the relationship Galen, and I had with what she had with Ben. One, Ben was a night vampire, so he couldn't be out during the day. And two, Galen didn't drink from me. She told me how much it turned her on and that it was the most amazing sex she'd ever had.

And yeah, I had that brewing over in my head. I won't be forgetting that information anytime soon. Maybe that was also a reason why Galen didn't want to drink from me last week. Because I would turn into a crazy horny rabbit and jump him. The thought brought a smile to my face.

It took forever for Ada to return, and when she did, she brought another woman with her. This one was young with short black hair that shaped her face perfectly. I loved it. When I turned back to Ada, her grin was off the charts. She was blushing and looked like she was about to break out into a musical number.

"Oh...I think someone has a huge crush," I sung, and her eyes snapped to me, telling me to shut it. I held my hands up and said, "Okay, okay. You can tell me later... about your big *crush*." I could see her cheeks get even pinker.

The new women closed the door behind her, turned to us, and chuckled, "Oh, you would be right. She's crushing hard." Ada spun and pointed her finger at her, then to her lips, signaling to be quiet.

"Shut it, you. This is Kiara. Remember I told you about her, Lexi? She is my sister Destiny's best friend. She was supposed to have her commitment ceremony this weekend, but it's been postponed with everything that's been going on here. But yeah, she has two...guys."

We all watched as she struggled with the word. What was going on...I growled to myself. *Galen*. He'd compelled her so she couldn't talk about shifters outside Pack Kiba, so she couldn't say it now. He should have done that in a way she could talk to everyone. Ugh.

"Hi, Kiara, come on in and join us for a girls' party, where we ignore the problems of the day and try and smile before everything turns to shit again." She perched herself on the edge of the bed. I could see Ada still looking confused.

"I really need to speak to *Galen*. Right *now*," I said in a slightly raised voice and smiled at them all like I wasn't crazy. I didn't want them to worry or get upset about what had happened. And that should hopefully get his attention if he wasn't in Alaric's office or his house that was.

CHAPTER 42
GALEN

The plans had been made, traps set, but we seemed outnumbered still. Most of our shifters were young. Or old. There weren't as many females, but they could protect the children. We were going to leave the older males at the house to protect the rest.

When Noah came and got me, telling me that Lexi was screaming out my name, I panicked. I didn't know what to expect when I got upstairs and into the room, we'd all taken turns at some time last night sleeping with her. When I saw she was safe, laughing with a few of the girls, Hazel being one of them, I felt like I could breathe. Well, as much as I could when I was surrounded by so many shifters.

She told me what the problem was, and how I had to fix it. As if I'd chosen to compel Ada and not that I was ordered to do so by Alaric. Did I wait to ask Alaric if it was alright to do this, no fuck him. I just did it and left them to their girls' day as they kept calling it, but it was good to see them all smiling and happy.

I could hear some Rawlins and Kiba shifters fighting while on patrol. That wasn't going to help our cause, if there was infighting, we were just as bad as the rogue wolves who seemed to be holding it all together better than we were. Kiba seemed to be the worst for this rival fighting. The young guy that Lexi saved last night, Huxley, he was pack Rawlins, and he'd volunteered to be with a Kenneally pack member.

We needed more Huxley's, who saw each other as equals. The shifters were all the same, didn't matter what pack they came from, they still bled red, shifted into wolves, and did everything else teenage boys did. This feud between them was stopping Kiba, all of them from growing strong together. I was just thankful that it was only the teenagers and not the adults who acted like this. They seemed to understand the need to put aside differences and come together.

"BEN, HOW DID YOU SLEEP?" I asked.

I'd wanted to speak to Lexi in private, but Hazel had come with her, she wanted to see Ben before we got ready to fight. It was understandable, they were a couple, and I was proud of my friend for finally finding someone. If anyone deserved love, it was Benedict. I was much older than he was, but we'd bonded many years ago and I would call him my closest friend. He was a good man, and a good vampire.

Outside, it was quiet...calm. You could feel it in the air, the tension thick like a fog settling over Kiba. Alaric was right, they would use tonight's full moon to attack. Shifters believed it made them stronger. I wasn't sure on this, as it had never been spoken of in Kiba before, and teenagers like to talk. But just in case, we needed more of an edge. Shelly was on her way, and she was bringing some of the pack Keene was a part of with her.

Hazel flinched when Ben took a seat beside her, but Lexi didn't move a muscle. I wondered if she was getting used to my faster speed, that Ben doing it didn't faze her.

"Lexi, I wanted to ask your permission to share your blood with Ben. I won't give him too much, but you might hear his thoughts. I don't know exactly how this works, but given that your blood does that for me, it might also do that to Ben now that he is close by."

She was nodding before I'd even finished talking.

"Do you need more? Fresh? I'm happy to do

whatever you need. If this will make you faster and stronger, then take as much as you need," she offered, and I knew that would be her answer. She would do anything to protect the ones she loved, her newfound family. Even if it meant someone would be inside her head, it was a small price to pay for the safety of others.

I wrapped my arms around her and kissed her gently.

"We will only take a little," I said. "I want you to be ready at the house. If we have any more victims like Huxley, I'd really like you to be there and ready. I know you can do this, because you're amazing. Once this is all long behind us, I was thinking we should go on a little holiday. Just you and me, since the boys can't leave the area. Vegas? Maybe Europe?"

She chuckled and placed a small kiss on my nose, before placing her forehead against mine. Her eye sparkled at my words.

"That sounds fun," she pulled back a little. "I've always wanted to go to Disneyland. I lived in LA for so long, but never had money to go."

I kissed her, "I promise that as soon as this is over, and I hopefully compel all the rogue shifters to leave and avoid you, then we'll go to Disneyland. And ride everything and eat all the cotton candy and be sick on the roller-coaster." She laughed and called me a dork. But agreed to eating all the cotton candy.

It was Ben that alerted me to the time. "We need to get going, Galen."

He was right, but first, I needed to make sure Lexi was safe. So I called Rafferty to escort her back to the main house with Hazel. When they had both left I turned to Ben.

"Let's get stronger. Just be careful of what you think about. Can't have you talking bad shit to my girl."

He chuckled, "yeah I'm pretty sure she would tell Hazel, so will leave the bad thoughts till this is all over." He clamped his hand down on my shoulder and I knew this was going to be hard, tough and dangerous. And I was just grateful to have my friend here. Fighting with me.

"Thank you again for coming." I patted his back and he replied. "Anytime."

CHAPTER 43
GALEN

We waited, in the trees, on the ground, and in the field that surrounded the Lovell house, but there was no movement. It'd been dark for hours, the full moon reaching its apex in the sky and still... the only movement I sensed was from our packs. I was starting to wonder if we had this all wrong. My fangs had descended, and I was on alert from being around all the shifters scents. Shelly had arrived with seven members of the Seattle pack. I'd been hoping for more, but that was eight extra bodies here at least.

"We will kick some ass." She was tiny but a little fire cracker like Lexi. Keene held onto her, he was worried for her. I smiled at him and nodded. I would make sure nothing happened to her. They moved into position, adding to our number surrounding the house.

"What do you think they're waiting for?" Nash asked me, and I wished I had the answer for that. If it wasn't a set time, like I assumed it would be, then I didn't know what it was they were waiting for. But it made sense based on how they'd attacked last night.

I heard a clicking sound come from far away, but it was there. A few shifters beside me heard it too, and they faced north, preparing for what was to come, unaware that the threat also loomed behind us.

There was an explosion, and my ears rang for a split moment before healing themselves, but it was enough time for them to get the jump on me. Three large, red wolves attacked me from behind. I turned just in time to block their bites, but they pushed me to the ground. I jumped up ready for them, and they didn't relent. They didn't take turns, they all attacked me as one. Their teeth reaching out for me again, over and over.

I understood their plan here, take down the vampires then the other shifters were a more even match. I hissed out, my fangs dripping the venom I needed to put them down once and for all. I waited for the right moment, they knew they had to be careful, if they didn't get Lexi's blood then they wouldn't come back from my bite.

I sensed Rafferty coming for me, his smaller form jumping through the air and landing on one of the wolves. I fought the other two, and they were strong, but I was stronger, faster now that I'd had Lexi's blood.

I hit one in the muzzle before kicking the other clean across the field. The move surprised even me, and I watched his body fly through the air.

"Give us the girl and all this will be over." The other had shifted back to speak to me, and I took the chance to break his leg, swinging a low kick and bringing him to the ground. He howled out in pain before he shifted back into a red wolf, his fur matted and unkept. These wolves had tried to kill Ben, and they'd tortured Rafferty for all those years. I wasn't going to let them just walk away. I was going to end them here, tonight.

More descended upon us, all red wolves, and it was as if Pack Russet was only targeting me and now Rafferty was caught in the crossfire, but he didn't stop, he was fighting alongside me, two packmates working together. He was a swift fighter and was holding his own until three of them took Rafferty down and pinned him, ripping into his flesh over and over, but I couldn't get to him. I kept calling for help, but it was me against four wolves. One grabbed my leg, and I hissed out as they flooded my system with shifter venom.

I could feel Lexi's blood running through my veins, protecting me from the venom, and was able to grab ahold of him long enough to bite, my teeth sinking into his flesh, his fur thick on my tongue. I injected him with my venom, hoping it would keep him down long enough to fight off the other three and get to Rafferty.

As soon as I stood, I watched Rafferty's body go limp and saw nothing but red. They were going to fucking die for this. I could hear his heart beating, so he was still alive, but he needed help. I wasn't sure what they did to him, but he wasn't healing. I would protect him. He was my family.

"You're gonna wish you were all fucking dead," I screamed as I charged the nearest wolf. He crumpled beneath my arms as another bit my shoulder, injecting me with venom again. I spun and threw him off, but it was burning my veins, the blood was taking too long to stop this. I was slower now, I tried to get to Rafferty only to have two more sets of teeth on me, I didn't scream as their teeth ripped and the venom flowed. I struggled to get away from them. It was as if Lexi's blood was only able to work so much before it was all used up. And these shifters...they knew it.

Over and over, they bit me, my body screaming in pain. My veins on fire, I used the last of my energy to scream out to Rafferty, to "get up and run, protect Lexi." When I glanced back over to where he'd fallen, he was gone, and I felt a sense of relief wash through me. I'd distracted them long enough for him to heal and go to her.

I tried to scream out for back up, but nothing came out, until all I could hear was the ringing in my ears. My sight was fading until I couldn't see, only feel the ripping at my arms and legs. I slumped to the ground, thinking only of Lexi. My beautiful, smart, and badass Alexis Turner. The angel I never saw coming, but I was sure glad she had. I wanted her to know how much I loved her, and that I would always love her.

I have heard by many that in your final moments, your life flashes before your eyes.

That everything becomes clear, that this was the natural way of life and death for humans.

I didn't see my life, only regrets. And there were many.

But saving Lexi, that was the only thing I got right in my three hundred and twelve years. She awakened something in me, and I'd only just started really living. But saving her...it was worth the pain. It was worth everything.

"I LOVE YOU, Lexi. You have my heart, always and forever."

CHAPTER 44
LEXI

Something was wrong, I could feel it in my bones. We'd heard the fighting, and it was closer than I was expecting. I'd hoped that it wouldn't come so close to the house. I'd sat with Josh, singing some songs with him, and I'd promised him if he stayed in the movie room with all the other kids, that I would make sure he got to watch *The Avengers* with me when everything was back to normal. That helped to calm his nerves. Grayson and Jack were out there fighting, like all the other able men were.

We did have female shifters, but not many. Huxley was here, since he was told to protect us. After his near-death last night, they'd thought it was best for him to stay here, and I knew it made Ada feel better with the way she couldn't keep her eyes off him.

She had towels and blankets stacked up ready to go, and now her and Kiara were setting up makeshift beds, and all I could do was stand there and watch. I could feel a sick sense of loss, but I didn't know how to help or what to do. I kept pacing, my hands tingling with that healing power, and I wanted to go out there. I could see some of what was going on from the kitchen window and I was frozen, watching it all unfold. I could hear the howling and screams for help.

And all I could do was stand here and wait, guilt building up higher. My breathing was fast, and I could stop my body from shaking, listening to them all fighting...for me.

"I love you, Lexi. You have my heart, always and forever." I gasped for air, and dropped to my knees onto the hard tiles, I gasped again and held my throat as I coughed then screamed out.

"Galen, Oh god. Something bad has happened to him. Someone help him. Please I could barely hear him. He needs help." I sobbed, this wasn't happening again, this wasn't how it was supposed to be. This was bullshit universe, why? Why give me these abilities then let him just die...

I FELT hands on my body, "Lexi, come have a seat and drink something. I am sure he is fine, he was with a whole heap of them." I choked back a sob. "There is nothing you can do right now. Please come. You're scaring me," Ada's voice was shaky, her face pale and her eyes darting around every time she heard someone scream. My heart wouldn't stop racing, and I was scared. I held her hands in mine, and she gave me a worried smile.

"Maybe, maybe he was just telling me he loved me. He drank my... he will be extra protected right?"

She rubbed my shoulders and pulled me into a hug, god I felt stupid, like I overreacted. He was just trying to tell me something sweet. I felt the horrible feeling leave my body, it left me trembling in Ada's arms a little longer than I wanted. We didn't have time for this and my head drama. I took a deep breath and plastered on a smile. Ada looked at me like she knew it wasn't real, but I didn't care. I wanted to change the subject.

"Ada, you should be a nurse, not a cop." She shook her head and chuckled. "You're so good at this. Look at all you've done," and Kiara agreed with me, but Ada shook her head again. I let out a defeated huff.

"I...I didn't take any classes for that. I've always thought I would be a cop, to help people. I never thought I could be a nurse. I thought blood and gore would scare me."

"You handled yourself pretty well last night, and

there was a lot of blood," I explained. "Galen can help. He'll get you into nursing school if you want." Because he was fine, he was coming through that door at any moment to tell me it was all over and we can go back to our regular lives.

She smiled and hugged me tight, and it didn't take long for men to start running into the house, screaming out for medical attention. My heart sank at the sight of one of them. This guy was only young, but he had so many bites, wolf and vampire. It wasn't just a fight, this almost seemed like *revenge*.

Ada's facial expression changed and she went straight into nurse mode. It was really fascinating to watch. "Get him over here, lay him down," she ordered, wiping as much blood off the young guy as she could, Kiara and another woman by her side. I watched, almost frozen in place, like I wasn't in my body. This was all happening around me and I wasn't really here. I didn't hear my name until Ada pulled on my hand.

"Lexi, I can't help him. Can you please help?" she pleaded, but this was a lot more than with Huxley. I could feel my hands tingling, but I was worried that I wouldn't have the strength to heal anyone else. Zara, Noah's mom came in the room and ushered me forward to him as I dropped to my knees beside him. Fuck, I think I used to ride the bus with him. He had to be no older than fifteen if that.

"It's too much, I don't know where to start," I

explained, but she held my shoulders and told me that I could do anything if I just put my mind to it, that I had her strength and that of the pack. My hands were both tingling with warmth as I placed them on his crumpled body, his heartbeat was so slow...so very weak. I focused on the vampire venom, but there was just so much and the pain, when it transferred to me, was jarring. I didn't think I could continue. It was like sticking your hand in a fire and being burnt, but having to keep it there to help him. I flinched, but held myself in position, gasping for breath over and over. I wanted to take all his pain away, but it came at a price. I could feel my body growing weak as more wounded shifters were coming in. I wouldn't be able to save them all. Tears fell as I tried so hard to hold on, but it was too much.

I threw myself back, and Zara caught me. "It's just...too much. I don't know if I can save him. I don't have that kind of... energy," I said as I tried so hard to sit up on my own. My limbs felt like lead, weighing them down to the floor.

"Blood? Lexi. Do you think your blood would heal them?" Ada asked, forgetting the one rule we had. Not that it made much difference they were here for my blood regardless. Ada held onto my face with one hand, while the other held a water bottle to my lips and I gulped down a few cold sips.

Shifters didn't drink blood, vampires did. My blood had healed Galen, and if that was the key to healing from shifter bites, then maybe she was onto something. I had thought that last night with Huxley but dismissed it. But there was only one way to find out.

"Get a knife," I whispered.

CHAPTER 45

LEXI

There were screams as another fallen wolf was brought inside, but the screaming was coming from Ada. I turned to see Noah carrying in the limp form of Huxley. How? He was protecting the children... "oh god." I screamed out. Were they that close to our door that they got in? I didn't understand. I felt dizzy and weak., nausea rose, and my stomach rolled.

Zara called out over and over, until someone replied that the children were safe, that Huxley had tried to stop some of them from breaking in and Noah was already there trying to stop them. But why was Noah on his own? Where was Saint? They were matched to fight together; my throat was tight and I couldn't breathe. I felt a sob rising in my chest again.

We had three packs fighting together as one,

plus some others from Pack Bardoul and Keene's pack, but it wasn't enough. We were outnumbered, and I didn't factor that in today. I just saw a huge gathering of wolf shifters and three vampires and I felt safe. Like we would be fine, this would end hours ago. But I was wrong.

We all were.

Ada dropped the knife to me as she ran over to Huxley. I looked down at the large kitchen knife as Zara reached for it. I stopped her.

"Zara, can you please help me sit up? I want to do this myself," I had to, as it was all I could do to help, and I would make this work. *It had too*. With the cold steel of the knife in my hand, Zara placed my arm over a large bowl that Kiara had brought, and she had towels... white towels. All I could think about was how bad I wanted my mates with me right in the moment. I needed the strength from the four of them to get me through tonight. Inside the living room, red stained all the white tiles, bedding, and towels, turning everything red and pink. So much blood, and I was about to add mine to it.

I closed my eyes and, with all my strength, cut through my wrist. The pain caused my body to shudder, and I felt the warm liquid running down my wrist and hand, into the bowl. Zara and Kiara kept telling me how great I was, how strong I was to do this on my own.

But I didn't feel strong, I felt so weak. There was

nothing I could do to stop this, if only I had run away sooner... not let Galen talk me back into coming here. All the "if onlys" hung there, choices I could have made that didn't lead to this. The massacre of Kiba, Rawlins and Kenneally packs.

When the blood started to slow, Kiara wrapped a towel around my arm. I felt lightheaded as I looked into the bowl. I'd given a lot of blood, and my body was healing itself, like I knew it would.

But was it enough to save them all?

CHAPTER 46
LEXI

I couldn't feel my body as it lay there crumbled in a heap. It was as if I was looking down on everyone, on the chaos around me, so many dying right before my eyes. Zara wiping a wet towel across my forehead, Ada racing back and forth trying to get the unconscious shifters to drink my blood. Noah was standing guard at the doors, looking over to Ada, she was covered in so much blood, sweat and tears as she raced to another shifter dying of a vampire bite. Begging him to drink my blood. I closed my eyes and felt myself drift back into my body.

The pain was so great as my body burned from the inside. At first, I thought it was from lack of blood, but I realized it was my healing power, working so hard to heal my body, and anyone near me, I didn't have to be touching them I could heal them. My mind drifted in and out of consciousness, trying to block out all the pain.

"Lexi, Lexi... We have to move. They're breaking in." My ears were buzzing as I tried to listen to Ada's words.

I wanted to tell her to leave me here. I wanted it to stop, my life wasn't worth all this...death. My whole life had been surrounded by death. My mom, the man I called dad. The man who was to adopt me, all dead. Was it all because of me? Because of the blood that ran through my veins? If so, I didn't want it, all of it. I didn't want to be an angel anymore. I wanted someone to take it back. I wanted to just live a normal life, one without death and sadness.

My body hummed, and I started to feel like myself once again. I pushed myself to standing, Zara helping me and took in the chaos all around me—wolves fighting panthers, a mountain lion ripping at the leg of a Kiba man as he screamed in pain. Everything was red as they slipped in their own blood.

This had to end. *Now.*

"They want me, Ada. This can be stopped."

She held onto my arm, crying and screaming at me to run with the others upstairs, but I couldn't. I grabbed her by the shoulders, everything was now clear to me what I had to do.

"Tell them I love them. I love you. Being here

was the best time in my whole life, and I will never forget you." Before she could respond, I ran, my bare feet slipping on the blood as I ran outside into the full moon's light. All around me, the fighting still continued, seeming as if it would never end. And it wouldn't end, not until they had me.

If they wanted me, they had to catch me first. I took off towards the trees, I had a plan, and it involved the cliffs overlooking the rocks below.

I screamed with everything I had, my voice hoarse and dry as I flew up through the trees. Over and under branches, the mud slowing me down. I fell to the ground when I heard a howl nearby, my heart thumping hard as I pressed on. This was the only way to end it. There was no way I could survive that fall. I wasn't like the shifters, I didn't heal that fast. My wrist was still leaking after the knife.

If I did this, my family would be safe, and no one could use my powers against them or anyone.

"Lexi... Come here, pretty girl."

My heart hammered in my chest at my name being called. I screamed as a figure burst through the trees and darted to the side as a wolf barreled through, cutting them off and sinking their teeth into the vampire while I kept going.

This was it. I was saving them all. I kept telling myself that, the tears making it harder to see. I wiped them away, but it didn't help. I couldn't stop crying. I'd only just started living. I didn't get enough time. I needed more time.

When the small clearing came into view, I slowed as I approached the end. The cold breeze from the sea sent chills through my body, my skin prickling, and I heaved in huge gulping breaths of air between the racking sobs.

This was it—the ultimate sacrifice.

I stood there, glancing up at the moon. It was tainted now, stained with the blood of my family and friends.

I heard low growls, then a roar came from behind me. I didn't want to look back, I knew they had found me. It didn't take long, since my blood would've called them here, and soon there would be more of them. At least with them drawn here, it gave everyone a fighting chance back at the Lovell house.

"Pretty girl, what are you doing over there? Come with us. We won't hurt you."

That I already knew. I took a step closer to the edge, the sounds of the waves crashing to the rocks below like a slow song, over and over.

"Come here. Don't be silly, girl."

I closed my eyes, listening to the wind as I stretched my arms out wide.

"Rafferty, Ranger, Maverick and Galen... you will

always have my heart." I whispered into the wind as I tipped myself forward. The wind on my face was strong as it whistled past my ears. This was the right thing to do.

I was an angel without wings, and now for the first time...I was flying.

CHAPTER 47

RANGER

Raff had taken Galen to be healed by Lexi, only to find she had left and the house was overrun by rogue shifters and vamps. I didn't wait for Galen, I raced as fast as my four legs could push me. I could hear Ada, she had Lexi's blood and would give it to Galen healing him, and once again, Lexi saved his life. And now, I needed to save hers. Mav was right behind me, howling out over and over, begging Lexi to stop. We were coming.

The clearing came into view as I watched Lexi drop from the cliff, my wolf crying out in pain. Galen ran to the cliff's edge, but Maverick grabbed him before he jumped on him, pinning him to the ground. The bear shifter roared before turning on us, batting Rafferty away like he was nothing but a toy. My wolf, angry, hurt, and devastated at the loss of his mate, jumped at him, ripping and tearing until a bright light flashed above. The bear fell to the ground under me, unmoving but his eyes, like he was frozen.

"Lexi?" Galen called out, his voice sounded almost relieved. My head turning to the light, I stared up in pure awe at large golden wings, glowing like the sun. I shifted back, as did Mav and Raff and just stared.

"Lex? Is that you?" was all I could muster. The light was so bright, I couldn't see clearly. When they landed on the ground in front of me, the glow lessened until it was a faint light around a man standing there, and draped in his arms was my Lex and my body almost crumbled beneath me at the sight. Her arm hung low by her side and she looked dazed, but it was her. I felt sick and relieved, my heart hammering as Galen stepped hesitantly up to the man and took Lex into his arms.

I moved up closer to them, as we watched the man with the golden wings.

"Lexi, oh god. Why would you do that? Why would you leave me?" Raff sobbed into her chest, and her hand stroked his hair. Mav was there too, holding onto her tightly.

I just... this was so much, and the night had already taken too much of a toll on me. I wasn't going to think about it. My feet moved to her, and she reached out for my hand, squeezing it tight.

"I'm so sorry, I just wanted to help you all. It was

the only way I could think to stop this. I'm so sorry," she pleaded to us, and my heart broke then for her. She didn't deserve this. So much bad had happened in such a short time and she was trying to do what she thought best. But it wasn't, it was never the answer. We would have worked this out.

Then the man, the angel, flew up and away without a word. Who was he and where did he go?

THE SUN WAS SLOWLY COMING up over the horizon. It was beautiful as we all sat together, holding each other, breathing in each other scents, and being grateful to be living one more day with each other, with Lex. My mate, my love.

"Sons," a loud voice from behind us called out, and I turned to see my father, Nash, Jett, and Lyell standing at the edge of the clearing. "It's over." The way his body sagged, I felt a need to reach out to him. This was so hard, this fight. But I would never want to be an alpha, that was hard. And I could tell that tonight was the hardest he had ever had to fight.

We hadn't heard any fighting after the angel left. The bear had disappeared while we were watching the sunrise, and I didn't want to worry where he had gone as he didn't come for us or make a sound. He was just gone. Holding Lex was more important than to worry where a bear shifter ended up.

I smelled him before he landed—the angel. I realized then that he smelled like a much stronger version of Lexi. But he didn't call to me as his mate. It was a little different, but not unpleasant.

Everyone watched as he stood before us, his eyes the color of amber, his hair a rich golden brown. He looked like he was Lexi's older brother. His large golden wings were on display again as he eyed us all, then he focused on Lex. His wings curled back behind him, and I just stared at him in awe. He was... an angel.

"Lexi Turner." His voice was smooth and almost hypnotic.

Galen and Raff helped her to stand, and she stared the angel down. Oh fuck, Lex. I wouldn't want to fight him.

"I am Tobias, I heard word from my sister that I had fathered a child and to find her here. But I am confused as to how..." Tobias looked to all of us. I could sense more of our pack were coming through the woods, but my father growled low, telling them to hold back.

"You're too young to be my dad," Lex responded. Tobias looked at her and smiled, then held out his hand, palm up.

"Please come here, Lexi." She stepped out from our protection, and Mav took a step forward with her, but Galen held him tight. She walked into the glowing ring of light around Tobias and took his hand. He closed his eyes, his head looking to the sky as Lex gasped.

"You are my child, but I do not understand. Your mother, Elizabeth Black,"

Lexi made a sound and nodded. "That was my mom's name. Elizabeth, Black was her maiden name." He dropped her hand and took a step back, almost as if he was examining Lexi.

"Was... Is there something wrong? Did you know about me?" she asked, but it sounded as if she was full of sadness.

His eyes landed on mine and I stood taller, then they drifted to Raff, then Mav, and finally to Galen.

"I did not know, or I would have been with you. I still do not understand how. Where is your mother now?"

Oh god...

CHAPTER 48

LEXI

"Where is your mother now?"

My heart couldn't take all of this in. He was my father, this man with amber eyes, the same color hair, and who didn't look a day over twenty-five, if that. My mother...

"She's dead," I told him. There was no other way to tell him. Just she was dead.

I could see the flash of hurt in his eyes, I wasn't sure if it was for my mother or me.

"She died when I was five. I lived in foster care after that, until now. Now I'm here, with my family. My mates."

He kept looking back at them, I worried about what he was going to say next. Like did he disapproved of my mates.

"You have wolf shifters and a daylight vampire as mates?" he questioned, and I nodded but I could feel the thick lump forming in my throat. I didn't care if he didn't like them. Just because we shared the same DNA, didn't make him my father. You had to earn that title with me.

But he didn't say anything further. He just nodded and looked down to me again, his hand went to his chin as he tilted his head. His eyes not reaching mine, it was if he was thinking. But I could build up the rising panic in my chest he spoke.

"I still do not understand how Elizabeth birthed a child. *My child*. That is just unheard of."

I heard movement behind me, then Galen asked, "because you're an angel?" Tobias looked to Galen, then back to me. His eyes were swirling again, and I wondered if they always did that and if mine would too. It was almost like looking in a mirror. I had his eyes. He cleared his throat.

"My father is an angel, and my mother was... a wolf shifter. She was one of the only females born before—" Everyone gasped, and I think I almost fainted. His mother was a wolf shifter, his father an angel. "I can father children with any living being. But this does not answer the question as to how Elizabeth had my child."

"Why?" I asked, what was so wrong with my mom being pregnant with me, because that made no sense if he can father children. Why couldn't she have had his child? She was a human, the scientists back in Bardoul tested her DNA, they said she was human. So yes, she could have half angel wolf shifter babies too.

"Because, my child," he leant down and gently touched my shoulder.

"Elizabeth was a vampire."

RISING SUN... book 3 and the final book in the New Moon series.

ALSO BY BELLE HARPER

OUT NOW

Lexi is an angel, her father is too. But how was her mother... a vampire?

OUT NOW

My whole life, all I wished for was a best friend and a boyfriend who treated me like a princess.

Well for me, living in a small community where everyone knows everyone. And everyone knew me as the "annoying" girl, it was hard for me to get even one of those wishes.

But when new girl Lexi Turner strolled into English class and sat next to me. My wish finally came true.

For the first time, in eighteen years. Me. Ada Stephens, had a best friend.

Lexi wasn't a regular new girl who blended into the background. No, she was turning every male head in the high school, especially the Kiba boys. Ugh... they were so hot and knew it.

But they didn't hold a flame to Saint Wood. He graduated last year and I never stopped crushing... how could you.

He was Saint-freaking-Wood.

Now I had the bestie, I was just missing the one other thing I wished for.

Only... I think I wished a little too hard.

But not everything is what it seems. The Kiba boys held secrets... ones I shouldn't have known.

BELLE'S BOOKS

Rebels of Ridgecrest High

Reverse Harem ~ Enemies to Lovers

The Pact

The Lie

The Game

The Win

Omegaverse Standalone Series

Reverse Harem ~ Standalone

Harley

Storm ~ coming 2024

Paranormal Reverse Harem

New Moon Series ~Lexi~

Twice Bitten

Blood Moon

Rising Sun

Full Moon Series ~Ada~

Fallen Wolf

Torn Mate

Shifting Sun

Pack Kiba Novels/Novellas

Midnight Prince

Shadow Wolf

Contemporary Standalones

Naughty and Nice ~Christmas Novella

The Christmas Dunk ~ Coming November 2024

ABOUT THE AUTHOR

Belle is an Artist, Author, Wife and Mother.

She has an addiction to reading, notebooks, coloured pens and mint chocolate. She lives in the beautiful Australian bush, surrounded by wildlife and the smell of eucalyptus trees.

She also has a strong love for all 60's music, believes she was born in the wrong era and should have been at Woodstock.

If you would like to find out more about Belle, please come like and follow her:

Click Here to Like Belle's Facebook Page

Join Belle in her Facebook Group

www.authorbelleharper.com

Sign up to my Newsletter to keep up to date with my new Releases, Free Books and Giveaways.

https://www.subscribepage.com/belleharper

www.ingramcontent.com/pod-product-compliance
Lightning Source LLC
Chambersburg PA
CBHW071917130726
47909CB00014B/2060